OF A STRANGE
WORLD MADE

ANTHONY W. EICHENLAUB

This book is dedicated to Mary Shelly, who won the greatest story contest of all and brought the science fiction genre to life.

CHAPTER ONE

ASH MORGAN SWISHED from table to table in the little cantina, her yellow skirt a comet's tail to her brighter yellow tunic. She kept her tone light and her smile cheery as she mingled amongst the gray-clad colonists, acting as if the coin in her skirt pocket didn't carry the whole weight of its three-hundred-year journey from Earth. Here on Sky the penny represented to her all that humanity left behind, and she could think of nothing more precious.

She quelled the nervous tickle in her belly with a pull of nectar. These were her friends and fellow colonists. She could trade treasures with a friend, couldn't she?

"Are Simon and Hector looking this way?" Ash asked a woman twice her age.

"They can hardly help it."

Ash didn't know what that meant, so she took a long drink and moved to the bar. For a moment, she swayed to the morose tunes of the band, shuddering as the raw emotion settled deep into her bones. The band wasn't what she'd call great, but it was a long and serious walk from bad. She paid for a refill on her nectar, even though her head already bobbed on its own syncopated rhythm.

It was a fair enough trade, she told herself, but it might take some convincing. After forcing herself to take two deep breaths, she decided it was time.

No, not yet. Could she really make this trade? She dreamed of a day when she could watch Earth shows and read Earth books without suffering through the glitches that tech suffered down here on the planet. Ash took a swallow of her nectar, its sweet courage flowing down into her belly.

She slapped the copper coin down right on the paper flyer in the center of Simon and Hector's table, her hand covering the magnificent treasure as if she didn't even trust the two men to look at it.

"Here it is, gentlemen." She looked into the eyes of both men across the table. "As promised, a penny journeyed all the way from Earth." She revealed the penny with a flourish. "That there's genuine Earth copper. You didn't believe my ancestors passed it down to me, but there it is."

She took another sip from a glass of nectar while the two considered her treasure. The green fluid tasted of apples and had a healthy kick that some-times made her head spontaneously simulate catastrophic shuttle landings. The stuff was cheap here on the surface of Sky now that the bio lab figured out how to engineer the pitcher plants that extrude it. *Her* bio lab. She had only joined the scientists a year ago, but she already felt great pride in being part of the team. It wasn't easy making plants survive the low nitrogen atmosphere and inorganic soil, but they'd done it—at least on a small scale.

The little cantina curved along the outer arc of the colony's Commons building. It had a bar made of printed fiber, behind which Orson, the gray-haired barkeep, cheerily chatted up colonists. Orson wore a colorful red and black dashiki that contrasted hard against the severe gray styling of the cantina. She always wondered why more colonists didn't get more creative with their clothes, since it cost nothing to add color and style. Well, it cost time, and sometimes humiliating embarrassment when the only wearable clothes she had were hot pink jumpers or that one wrap that was supposed to stay tied but never quite did.

Simon, a year older than her but still barely old enough to take seriously, crossed his arms and frowned. "It's not real," he said. Simon liked to vary his wardrobe, eschewing boring shirts for stylish cuts in a staggering array of grays. The loose-fitting suits he wore drowned his skinny frame, but his meticulously styled, dapper hair flopped off to one side and made Ash's elbow-length mass a tiny bit jealous. *Ash* wasn't jealous, though—not of Simon.

Ash poked Simon in the chest. "How would you know? Your Earth History grades nearly got you stuck on the ship." She felt a little bad turning Simon's fantastically weak self-confidence against him, but there it was.

He didn't cave so easily. "You printed a replica down at the mids." Simon referred to the mid-sized printers, which could have printed something similar, but not quite. "And I'm a cultural archivist. My Earth grades were fantastic."

The room grew quiet as the band took a break between sets. The reedy instruments gave Ash a mild headache, but silence itched at her like an old radiation burn. She fidgeted in her seat. Her gaze fell to the flyer under the penny, which invited her to participate in a story-writing contest. The contest was Simon's project—something to do with establishing cultural norms. She took another sip knowing full well that someone of her slight stature didn't need to drink all that much to get genuinely drunk. Fortunately, she was already too tipsy to care.

"Do we have a deal or what?" Ash asked.

Next to Simon sat Hector, who was a year younger than her but twice as big. He wore the standard colonist garb: plain gray shirt and plain gray pants. Hector was one of the latest additions to the colony, just shuttled down six months prior in order to run heavy equipment for a construction project. His big belly shook in what Ash took to be a silent laugh. He reached out a meaty finger to touch the little coin, but Ash slapped his hand away with a loud snap.

"Leave it, Hector. This is a no touching show."

Hector narrowed his eyes. "How do I know it's worth anything?"

Ash threw up her hands in mock distress. "Worth anything? Do you even know what this is? This is a genuine, honest-to-god true, real United States penny. These were worth a fortune back on Earth. According to my Granny Aspen, her great, great grandmother snuck this here coin onto the colony ship when they boarded up off of Earth. This here—" She leaned in really close and squinted at the coin. "This is a two thousand fifty-six. Says there right on the front. This was the last year anyone ever made pennies, which makes this particular one extra rare. Back on Earth, one of these shiny pennies could be traded for an automobile." When she saw the furrow of Simon's brow, she explained, "The automobile was like a spider walker, but with wheels instead of legs."

"And they didn't print whole buildings like our walkers do," Hector said.

Ash nodded, a little impressed that the big man knew anything about cars. She slapped him on the shoulder a little harder than intended. Wow, that was a lot of muscle. She left her hand there significantly longer than might be socially appropriate. "Smart man," she said.

Simon nodded, as if automobiles were obviously something he had already heard about a million times. He probably cheated to get passing Earth History grades. "I don't think it's a real penny."

Ash scowled as hard as she could, the effect ruined when she took a sip from her drink. "You calling Granny Aspen a liar?"

Simon let out a sigh. "No, Ash. I'm calling *you* a liar. Remember when you brought us what you called a live frog that you said you'd printed whole in the bio printer?"

"It was alive for a little bit!"

Hector scratched his chin. "I thought nobody ever printed more than a few live cells at a time."

"I swear it was alive!" It had been. Briefly. Well, sort of. "I mean, it had an electric pacemaker, but it swam like it was alive."

Simon shook his head. "You mean it twitched in the water and kinda moved when you shocked it."

Hector shuddered and shot Ash a worried look that she didn't much appreciate.

When Ash had nothing else to say, Simon said, "Do you remember the so-called alien tech?"

Ash took a big gulp of her nectar. "It wouldn't be alien." Was her voice slurring? "*We're* the aliens here, remember. If there was strange tech here on planet, it'd be from natives."

"But there wasn't, because nothing lives on this planet but us." Simon said. "You made the whole thing up."

Ash had exaggerated on that one. She hadn't exactly found the strange device, but she had thought it up and it had seemed really strange. Could she help it if they got the wrong idea and made a big deal out of it? Nobody could really blame her if she happened to wager it against Simon's legendary glitchless tablet. He had brought it down from the colony ship, and it meant a lot to him. No way was he going to wager it against something he thought Ash could just reproduce in a few hours of printer time. She'd lost the stupid chess game, anyway.

"It could have been real," she said. "And that has nothing to do with this deal."

"You really want my tablet, don't you?"

"It's a fair deal." Ash wanted that tablet. "A penny from Earth is worth way more than that tablet and you know it."

Simon drummed his fingers on the table, as if considering the trade. "No deal."

Ash threw up her hands.

"Face it, Ash," Simon said. "You're too much of a storyteller."

Ash blinked at him. She was certain he was going to call her a liar again. She took a big gulp of nectar. "Writers are stupid. Every good story's already been told, so why bother?"

Simon snorted. Actually snorted! "By people on Earth?"

Ash looked to Hector for help but got none.

Traitor. "By people on Earth. Smart people, like Shakespeare and Stephen King and that guy with all the six-toed cats."

"Ernest Hemingway?" Hector asked.

Simon smiled, and Ash didn't like his smirk one bit. "You're right, there's no way you could write a better story than Hector or me."

Ash bristled. She stood up and pointed a finger at Simon. The room swayed, and she wasn't entirely sure she was pointing straight at him, but she spoke, anyway. "You wanna bet on that?" Then, she sat down because she was probably going down anyway and sitting seemed like the most graceful option.

"Ash," Simon said with phony sincerity. "Hector and I have been working on our stories already. Do you really think you can beat us?"

Ash marveled at her empty cup as Orson refilled it. She took another sip, but her lips were numb and that probably wasn't a good sign. She squinted at the flyer. The contest had been going for almost four months already and would complete in less than a week. "I'll wager my penny," she slurred, "because I know I'm going to win."

Hector shook his head sadly.

Ash scowled at him. "Did you say Hemingway?"

"I'll wager the tablet," Simon said. "I don't want to risk losing it, but it's not really much of a risk, is it?"

Ash made a slow turn, moving her scathing gaze

from Hector to the unfortunate Simon. She spoke slowly so he would understand, and, also, because she wasn't sure she could string together a sentence very quickly in her current state. "When I was on ship, I watched every movie from the Earth archives, and I read most of the good books. If anybody in this colony knows stories, it's gonna be me."

"You think so?" Simon shook his head.

Ash stuck a thumb at her chest. "That's right, I'm going to win, and I've been working for months on my story." She hadn't. "Put your money where your mouth is, Simon." He already had. "You too, Hector." She honestly couldn't remember if he had or not. Ash stood and addressed the entire cantina, which, admittedly, was only about a dozen drab colonists. They looked up at her from their own drinks, amusement shining in their eyes. It wasn't often they got to see someone make such a spectacle. "Everybody," Ash said, "hear this: Simon, Hector, and I are making a bet. Whoever writes the best story of us three gets—" the room swayed around her, but she stayed on her feet "—Hector's steel knife, Simon's tablet, and a brilliant, copper penny from Earth."

Ash flopped back down into her chair.

Simon pushed his tablet into the center of the table. Hector unclipped his knife from his belt and set it on the tablet. He'd forged it himself, and it held a much better edge than anything the printers could make.

"We have a bet, then." Ash reached out to pick up her penny.

"Ah, no." Simon blocked her. "Orson, will you keep these things in escrow for us?" He didn't take his eyes off of Ash. "We want to make sure there isn't any funny business with the items in our little wager."

The barkeep gathered the three things, nodding appreciatively at the knife, but for some reason ignoring the sheer beauty of polished copper. "I'll keep them in the display, then," he said. With a key on his belt, he unlocked a glass box, which held a few other trinkets from the old world. The faded Babe Ruth rookie card and fist-sized sapphire would need to make room until the three of them came up with their stories.

The band started playing again, so Ash left the cantina, taking a moment at the door to verify that the walls were, indeed, propped up. They swayed back and forth, but no, they weren't going to fall over after all.

Yes, they were. Ash stumbled a few feet to collapse on a short bench. The fibrous material flexed a little under her body, even though her skinny frame had to be the lightest thing it had held all week. Ash pulled her hair back into a ponytail, tying it with a strip of purple cloth she'd printed in her lab.

This spot claimed one of the best views from the colony of Edge, which somebody had named for the way it sat at the edge of the world looking off into the broken sky. Ash wondered if that same person had named the planet Sky, out of some odd sense of irony. Her drunk brain couldn't focus on that for long. Not with that fantastic view splayed out before her. The squat, functional buildings radiated out from the Commons, clustering in areas where industry met the residential. Most buildings bore a single lightning rod as decoration, necessary for the upcoming storm. Now, by the light of five of the seven moons, Ash could make out the silhouette of the lab where she worked very, very early the next morning.

Edge sat on the side of a high mountain, high up where the planet's oxygen-heavy atmosphere thinned enough for the colonists to live at an acceptable level of comfort. Beyond the mountain lay a vast ocean, it's waters churning from the single, massive storm that circled all of Sky.

The air tasted sour on Ash's numb lips, so she drew up her rebreather from where it hung around her neck. Its clear mask sat close to her face, not forming a tight seal, but adapting the air she breathed through controlled airflow. Colonists were supposed to wear rebreathers at all times, but nobody wore them indoors where filters pulled most of the grit from the air. Breathing the purified air through her mouth steadied her head a little, even if it did taste like plastic. Due to some trick of chemistry, Sky had plenty of oxygen. Too much, really,

but the colonists had all been hardened against the
dangers of over-oxygenation thanks to their ancestors' hundreds of years of preparation on the generation ship. Granny Aspen's great, great grandmother
probably would have passed out with this much
oxygen. Ash only got a little lightheaded. The
rebreather helped.

Ash closed her eyes and rested her head against
the building. In a few minutes, she would walk
across town, but a short rest never did anyone any
harm. She kept her eyes closed when her bench
creaked under someone else's weight.

"Ima kick your ass, Simon," she said, still
slurring.

A woman's voice responded. "You're Ash,
right?"

Ash opened one eye to peer sideways at the
woman. She had a ratty nest of dark hair, loose gray
clothing, and a haunted look that Ash had come to
associate with the overworked techs in one of the
many labs. The woman was also in a very advanced
stage of pregnancy. Ash closed her eyes again. A
wave of nausea rolled over her.

The woman swallowed, her throat making an
audible click. "I'm Marta," she said.

Ash squinted at her. She remembered the
woman. Marta had been on one of the first waves of
colonists to descend upon Sky.

Marta clutched Ash's arm. "I thought you might

help me. Your—your mother was a midwife for your borough on the ship, right?"

"It's not a hereditary trait."

The woman waited a few breaths before responding. She didn't wear a rebreather, and her lips were dry and cracked. "If you help me, I can make it worth your while."

Ash opened her eyes too fast, prompting another wave of nausea. The moonlight washed over the two of them, and a cool breeze blew from the south.

"I work in the med lab," said the woman in a flat voice. "There are some recreational drugs I know how to print."

"That's not allowed."

Marta rested her hands on her belly. "True."

Ash looked at the woman, taking in her full cheeks and dark expression. There were midwives and doctors in the colony. Plenty of them, really. Ash's mother still lived on the ship, but others had come down with the colony. "I know there's precisely zero chance you're carrying an unlicensed baby. Ain't nobody that stupid, is there?"

The woman's jaw tightened. "I'm just asking for help during the delivery," she said. "Not your judgment."

Even if Ash helped this lady, the baby would never find a place in the community. Resources were tight on this barren rock, and the colony's artificial intelligence, Traverse, managed population closely. It had to.

Or else.

Nobody ever said anything after, "Or else."

"Excuse me?" Marta asked. Ash wondered if she had spoken aloud. "I have a place past the quarry," the woman said. "It's safe there, and none of the automated systems will find me. I can take care of the baby on my own, but I want some help for this."

"Traverse will never let your baby live."

Marta grabbed Ash's arm hard enough to leave bruises. "You don't understand," she said. "These draconian restrictions won't last. There are break-throughs every day. You know better than anyone that multi-cellular flora's almost self-sustaining." She blinked back tears. "And my boy is special."

Ash stood, pulling her arm away from the woman. She had already offended the automated systems enough to know how unpleasant life could be. She stared at the dark distance over a hundred miles of open ocean. Clouds smudged the far hori-zon, lit by the far-off flash of lightning that gave this planet its most beautiful and dangerous feature. The lightning storm circled the globe, and in less than a week it would pass over Edge without pause or mercy. Ash couldn't afford the disdain of the AI when that hit. Not if she wanted to write her story and get the best of Hector and Simon.

Her head no longer swayed from the drink. "I'm sorry," she said to the woman. "Find someone else."

With that, Ash walked home.

CHAPTER TWO

THE NEXT MORNING, Ash worked her lab equipment through the blood-thick haze of a pounding headache. She wore Earth clothing: an ankle-length orange pleated skirt and a long-sleeve Pink Floyd shirt. Between long bouts of hangover-induced regret, Ash wondered if some of the throbbing pain in her head wasn't a longing for a home world she would never see.

Life must have been so much better on Earth, where the cities were hotbeds of a thriving humanity. The whole planet crawled with art and architecture. A traveler could experience ten thousand years' history in its museums and archeological sites. On Sky, there was nothing. No history, no art, no culture—no humanity.

"Anyway," said her always-energetic lab partner, Olympia, "when he said he was going to give me flowers, I figured he'd grow them himself all the way up from a single cell, and that sounds romantic, right? Well, he didn't." The way Olympia's dreadlocks danced across the shoulders of her gray jumper when she shook her head made Ash's stomach churn.

Ash swiped across her printer controls, loading up the jobs she'd queued up the previous day. The desk-sized machine hummed and emitted the ozone glow of the origin of synthetic life.

Olympia frowned. "Instead, he went down to the mids and printed out fake plastic flowers. Can you believe that? He's trying to flirt with one of the colony's best exobotanists and all he can do is bring a pile of printed flowers? They were gray!"

Ash blinked, her eyelids sheets of dry sandpaper. She had no idea who Olympia was talking about. "He didn't," she said.

"He did!" Olympia carried a pile of petri dishes from their shared station, loading them into an incubator the size of a large wardrobe. Each dish slotted into a climate-controlled space. "And he was all proud of himself. Said he was an artist."

"What did you do?" Ash didn't care *at all* what Olympia had done, but she knew from experiences that these conversations lingered until they'd dropped their steaming gossipy payload, and sometimes they didn't move forward without a solid push.

Olympia took one of Ash's hands in both of hers, and leaned close to whisper, "I kissed him."

"Even though he gave you fake flowers?"

Olympia shrugged. "He's cute. Plus, what else is an artist good for?"

The printer dinged, and a door slid open along the side. Ash drew a slide out of the central container and locked it under the microscope. On the screen, she maneuvered the device into focus so that she could see how her programming had held up. The single printed pseudocell sat suspended in a drop of nutrient auger, rotating slightly from the movement. Its organelles showed in sharp contrast against the gray background, and all appeared intact. The rush of joy fought back her headache. She pumped her fist, and the movement sent the agony tumbling back like an upended box of beakers.

"Good?" Olympia asked.

Ash took the slide out and moved the cell into a petri dish. "Make sure this one gets plenty of oxygen. It'll thrive in slightly higher concentrations than background. And five degrees warmer than average, too, if you can."

Olympia carried the tray to the incubator as if it might be a ticking bomb. She slid it into a slot and programmed the required parameters while Ash clutched her skull between her hands and squeezed her eyes shut in an attempt to keep from vomiting.

"Is this one something special?" Olympia said, ignoring her pathetic partner's plight.

"This is the one that'll scrub the atmosphere," Ash said. "If it works, it's light enough to float in the wind, feeds mostly on sunlight, oxygen, and particulates, and in late stages of its life it'll cluster up and fall like a rain of blue petals to build an organic component into the soil. If the oxygen levels ever drop significantly it'll stop thriving, so we shouldn't have to worry about it making the planet uninhabitable."

"Shouldn't?"

Ash pressed her palms against her eyes to ease the throbbing. "I've been testing variations on this for months, but it seems like forever." Terraforming was dangerous, especially on a planet that already had a stable oxygen supply. One wrong organism could suck up all that tasty oxygen and render the planet uninhabitable. Ash thought of all the many ways her new organism could go wrong, and it paralyzed her. Once her creation left the lab, it might do anything.

Ash queued up the next bio print job. It would be another variation on the pitcher plant, hopefully something that wouldn't cause such terrible hangovers. As she worked, she started to think about writing her story.

Stories writhed around in her head like a bucket of slippery eels. What kind of story did she want to tell? What era of Earth history would be the best focus? Simon thought stories should be new, but Ash knew better than that. Nothing interesting ever, ever happened on Sky. She could tell a story from a classic series like M*A*S*H, or a realistic one from a show like Friends. Those were some of her favorites. What about the work of Anton Chekhov? His stories were short and powerful, and they illustrated an important period of Earth history. She rubbed her temples and rested her head on the lab table. There were too many stories, and they weren't helping her think of what to write at all.

When Ash looked up, Olympia had already left for lunch. The sticky crust over Ash's eyes hinted that she might have dozed off. Marta's optimism came back to her through the hangover fog. The pregnant woman had been convinced something would happen soon, but even with Ash's potential breakthrough, resources would be tight for years. How long could Marta hope to keep her baby hidden? Guilt gnawed at her gut worse than any hangover.

"Traverse," she said to the computer. "Give me colony status."

Her screen went blank for a second, followed by a mangled stream of statistics. Ash squinted as if that might help her decipher the distorted figures. Every screen in Edge had this glitch where letters and numbers came up wrong. She liked to think she was pretty good at deciphering the meanings.

Population held steady at two thousand, with food and water stores good for almost a year. That seemed stable enough. Broken down into component nutrients, Ash could tell that iron and zinc were in short supply. That might limit reproduction, but there were ways to close that gap chemically. In the corner of the screen, Travers's logo spun in a graphic display: a T rendered in a color that Olympia always described as phosphorescent lime.

"Two thousand's a suspicious number, Traverse," she said. "Doesn't that seem a bit round to you?"

"Two thousand is the designated population limit for the given resources."

"What would one more baby do to the colony, Traverse?"

The screen showed the images of three women. Marta was not on the list. "Three children are expected in the colony to replace retiring older persons. Current production can sustain all three with minimal difficulty."

"What if there were another one?"

Traverse paused for several seconds. "Unauthorized pregnancies are aborted."

Of course. Ash's mother had always taught her that the needs of the colony outweighed the needs of the individual. She'd never forget her mother's haunted look as she'd described how important contraceptives were. Coming from a midwife who's only job was bringing life into the world, the message seemed almost hypocritical. But back then, the population cap was close to its limit aboard the ship. Here on the colony, resources were more flexible. The rules should have changed.

She glanced at the clock on her screen. The ship

would be overhead, its massive solar sails eclipsing the sun.

"Traverse," she said. "I would like to speak with my mother."

Traverse's logo grew to overtake the entire screen and spun in silence for several seconds. When Ash was about to doubt the connection, the logo disappeared, replaced by the image of Ash's mother.

Kamala Morgan held the kind of vibrant energy that defied age. Her gray eyes sparkled with joy and warmth, and every time Ash talked to her, a red-hot lump of homesick lodged itself in her heart. Kamala held an ebony tablet in her right hand and gestured loosely with her left. "How are things on the surface, sweetling?"

Ash hated being called sweetling but refused to take the bait. "Hey, Mom." She spoke with as much warmth and enthusiasm as her hangover would allow, which wasn't much. "You know all the rules about unauthorized babies, right?"

After a slight delay for transmission lag, Kamala's eyes widened. "Ashley, dear. Are you pregnant?"

Ash shook her head and said "No," a little too vigorously. "It's not me."

"My goodness, dear. Don't they supply you with contraceptives down there? How are supplies? Are they starving you?"

"Mom."

"Do you know who the father is?"

"Mom!"

Kamala disappeared from the screen, and her off-camera voice came through muffled. "Garland, dear, Ash is pregnant."

Ash threw her hands in the air. "I'm not pregnant!" She tapped hard on the screen. Every interaction with her mother over the screen made her wish so badly that she could touch her mother: either to hug her or to grab her by the shoulders to shake her. Mostly the latter. "Someone I know is pregnant."

Kamala appeared on the screen. "Certainly, dear." She didn't sound convinced.

"I want to know what the rules are. How does Traverse decide who to keep?"

"Unauthorized pregnancies are aborted, sweetling." Same stupid thing the AI had said.

Ash ground her teeth and pinched the bridge of her nose. "But what if they're not. What if someone manages to bring one to term?"

Her mother didn't respond for what felt like an eternity. Her eyes grew unfocused, and the lines at the corners of her eyes deepened. Finally, she said, "We almost hit a population limit up here not long ago."

"What did you do?"

Kamala's expression did not change. "We sent five hundred of you down to the planet."

"Thanks, Mom." Ash was silent for a long time, studying her mother's face. She only wished that she could properly make eye contact through the screen, but no matter what they did, they always seemed to miss each other.

"Your father has been quite busy lately," Kamala said to break the silence. "He's started playing squash every morning."

"You told me that last week, Mom."

"Yes, well, it's a big deal to us." Kamala's eyebrows knitted together with worry. "We're doing fine up here, dear."

"I know. I love you, Mom." Ash cut the connection and rested her head on the desk. Marta's pleading looks haunted her when she closed her eyes. Ash told herself over and over not to feel guilty about letting the woman fend for herself, but it didn't work.

"Traverse," she said. "What would it take to let population grow by one in the colony?"

"Population is at a maximum."

Stupid AI. Ash knew it wasn't a real person, but she'd learned to hate it, anyway. It kept the colony alive with its strict adherence to the laws, but those same laws stole freedom from them on a daily basis. Some Earth cultures had lived under oppression, but at least they had hope of revolution. And a person could flee to another country on Earth. Or fight. Ash's defiance felt like nothing in comparison to the great stories of Paul Revere or Che Guevara. Orson's cantina had a secret stash of nectar plants, just to meet the meager demand, and that was about as much rebellion as she had ever seen. Traverse was perfect for running a ship where the laws were an absolute necessity due to the closed system. A colony needed more freedom. Flexibility. Ash had volunteered to be on this colony mission just so she could get a little distance from all that rigidity.

On the ship she never met so many people as she saw in Edge. Her tiny borough aboard the ship had had limited communication with the others and never any physical visitation. They lived like a little village in the stars with an all-powerful beneficial dictator who happened to be the ship's AI. Funny how that dictator followed them down to the planet like a helicopter parent.

She wondered how long a baby could survive on smuggled nectar.

CHAPTER THREE

THE NEXT MORNING, Ash dressed in a t-shirt with a yellow smiley face on the back, bellbottoms, and a trench coat. The coat was too warm in the day's armpit humidity, but drastic shifts in temperature heralded the oncoming storm, and she wanted to be prepared. She took the time to print a new pair of work boots for the same reason, but they didn't fit right, so she switched back to her worn-out tennis shoes.

She took the day off of work and surreptitiously questioned some jittery med techs about Marta. Nobody had seen Marta in days, even weeks. What kind of isolation must the woman have gone through to hide her pregnancy?

"She's had a rough time," said a man with thick glasses and hair like a Monet haystack. "Ever since... Well, last couple years she's been in and out a lot."

A mousy girl a year younger than Ash said, "She

stopped wearing her rebreather outside, like it didn't even matter."

Ash gathered some things and set out to the north of Edge on foot, skirting the blasted crater of the quarry, where giant machines processed raw earth into constituent molecules for recombination. Ground shook as powerful colliders made feed for the printers: molecular building blocks for the very life she created in her lab as well as materials for their technology, their buildings, and their food. Smaller machines, the spider walkers, moved around the quarry gathering raw stone, later returning to the colony to print whole structures from their spinnerets. Everything the colonists had came straight from this quarry, and the very air shimmered with the raw power of their destruction.

The books said the color of Sky's sun was different from that over Earth, but Ash never knew the difference. It was the color she always knew, but the sun's sharp blue brilliance up in the sky didn't burn the way she knew the Earth sun did. It washed over the land with a cool intensity that refracted in the suspended particulates of the still atmosphere to form rainbows that swept across the sky. On the Eastern horizon, the storm approached. It flashed with yellow, the dark clouds a smudge atop a vast and barren sea.

The storm didn't worry Ash. She had lived through the storm twice before, and she knew she would many times again. It still lingered far off and would take days to reach Edge.

Beyond the quarry, the land grew untamed and rough. No roads stretched out this far since there were no other colonies and nothing much to see. Ash saw the occasional fresh hint of Marta's passing, in the boot print on the ground or a small pyramid of stones.

After walking an hour past the quarry, she turned around and couldn't see Edge at all. A brief swell of panic welled up in her. What if she couldn't find her way home? Ash sat on a broken stone, trying to control the gasping breaths that wouldn't stop.

Then, she heard the scream.

Ash ran. Her shoes crunched across the dry gravel as she descended the hill. The scream came again, and Ash knew it was Marta. It had to be. She raced downward and forward, unable to think about the risks.

The cave opened to the western sky, and Ash found herself upon it when she leapt down from a ridge into its open maw.

Marta wept, whether for joy or pain, Ash did not know. She followed the sound, eyes blind in the sudden darkness. The cave smelled of fresh, cloying sweat.

"I'm here," Ash said.

Marta's only response was to weep.

Ash drew a light stick from her pack and illuminated the little cave. Marta lay on the floor, a synthetic weave splayed under and around her like a pool of spilled paints. She'd stripped below the waist. Sweat matted her tangle of hair. Next to her sat a backpack and a small printer and battery pack.

"You came," Marta said.

"Mom always said it's hardly ever anything more than catching," Ash said. "I suppose I can help with that."

Marta ground her teeth. Ash wished she had brought some nectar.

The body knew its business and nine times out of ten it'd get it done. Ash hoped this wasn't the tenth time. She cleaned her hands with a sanitizer as she looked Marta over. How long had this woman been laboring here on her own? Hours? A day? Madness danced at the edges of the woman's eyes. When Ash took Marta's hand, the woman squeezed so hard Ash thought her fingers might break.

But the baby was close. It had already dropped, and Ash could only hope everything pointed the right direction.

Ash looked the other woman right in the eyes as the next contraction turned her belly into a ball of granite. "Not yet," Ash said. "Just breathe this time."

Marta forced a slow breath, quiet scream escaping as she did.

Slow, burning regret boiled in the pit of Ash's stomach. Ash felt the sense of a trap closing on her. Her decision to come out here irrevocably bound her to Marta's fate, and a deep piercing dread pressed slowly on the center of her chest.

When Marta's contraction passed, Ash quickly worked to make Marta more comfortable. "You're almost there," she said. "How long have you been out here?"

Marta gave a quick shake of her head, which could have meant she didn't want to say, or it could have meant she didn't know. How strangely time passed in the little cave. Before she knew it, contractions started again, and Marta choked back another scream.

"Slow and steady," Ash said, imitating the way she'd heard her mother say it so many years ago. "Slow breaths."

Several more contractions passed in this way, with Marta collapsing from exhaustion between them. Ash frantically fought the growing sense of futility that gnawed at the edges of her being. She was there to catch and to coach as best she could. While Marta did all the work, Ash could do nothing.

"My pack," Marta said in a quiet voice. "Get out the medbox."

The medbox was a smaller, portable version of the printers Ash worked with and contained a mix of free molecules used in the production of medicines. Where Ash's equipment could create life itself, Marta's could save it. Or possibly reduce pain.

"You're almost done," Ash said.

Marta ground her teeth. "It's too much," she said.

"A couple more pushes, that's all."

The woman grabbed Ash by the shirt and yanked her close down to her face. "Give me the box," she said through her teeth.

Marta fumbled with the box's console, activating a preprogrammed module. Three pills popped out. "Relaxants and painkillers," she said. "That's all."

"Why are there three of them?"

Marta grimaced. "Water," she said.

"It's just another couple pushes, that's all. You don't need pills for that."

Sweat and tears rolled down Marta's cheek. "It's too much," she said in a quiet voice.

Ash studied the three tiny pills in her hand. They all looked identical, which she thought was strange if they were really two different kinds of pills. Also, wouldn't pills take too long to affect the mother? Maybe they were fast-acting, but that would still take several minutes. As far as Ash could tell, the woman was only a contraction or two away.

"It's not too much, Marta." Ash took both of the woman's hands in her own. "You can do this."

Marta's hand closed around Ash's wrist. Her grip like a vice, the crazed woman squeezed until Ash relinquished the three pills.

Ash handed Marta a water pouch, and the mother-to-be swallowed the three pills. The next contraction hit like a crash of lightning. The thunder that followed rumbled and roiled at the woman's belly, even as she slipped close to unconsciousness.

"Stay with me, Marta," Ash said, repeating the woman's name as often as she could to keep her attention. Ash wondered what the woman had taken. "Marta, this is it. You're going to push, and then you'll be done."

The cave stank of blood and crap and life. Ash didn't know how long she had been in the timeless cave, struggling at the side of this exhausted woman.

When the next contraction came, Marta pushed. Ash bit her tongue, hands in position to catch. A black tuft of hair poked out, then more. The baby's red, scaly skull emerged, as if sensing its own freedom. Then it stopped.

Marta slumped back, her eyes closed. The rays of the setting sun shone through the cave entrance, slashing across Marta's face like a knife.

"No," Ash said. "Marta, keep pushing. You almost have it." She nudged Marta's leg, but the woman didn't wake. She couldn't get her fingers around the baby's head. She couldn't pull. Her mother had tools for this. A suction cup that sucked the baby out. What could she do?

Ash slapped Marta on the cheeks. Not even slapping woke her. The pills must have been too much, whatever they were. Ash touched the woman's belly, feeling in it for the baby. She pushed, leaning as hard as she could, but it wasn't enough.

The next contraction came, weaker this time. The oddly formed belly tensed into a boulder, and Ash pushed.

Marta's eyes snapped open, vibrant gray in the blue light. "A mistake," she said. "God almighty it was a mistake. Get this thing out of me!"

"You have to push," Ash said as she circled around to touch the baby's head. It grew pale under her fingers, bluish under black hair. "Push!"

Marta screamed, and the baby came free.

Ash's breath caught when she saw the baby's deformed face in the shadows, and the dread she had felt before finally had a home.

The baby didn't breathe, and for a short second that would haunt Ash's dreams forever, she wished that it would not. She held the hideous little creature, but not close to her body. Some instinct repulsed her. The wretched thing twisted and squirmed, threatening to fall from her grasp.

Then it squalled. *He* squalled.

"You have a boy," Ash said. She wiped the baby clean with a cloth.

Color returned to his strange face. Ash didn't get a good look at it in the cave's shadows, but something was wrong. Very wrong. She handed him to Marta, who was already unconscious again. The baby struggled to latch, but when it did, it stayed and the cave went quiet.

"Sleep," Ash said to the new mother. "The hard part has only just started."

Marta's face twisted under another contraction, and Ash worked the afterbirth free. It slid out without problem, and Ash drew a blanket from her pack to cover the sleeping woman. She clipped the umbilical cord, the same as she had seen her mother do many times. Marta didn't seem to be bleeding.

A dark shadow passed over Marta, and it took Ash a moment to realize that someone moved outside the mouth of the cave. They'd been found.

"Ash?" came Hector's voice, quivering with uncertainty. "Ash, is that you in there?"

If Hector reported back about the baby, they would never find the resources to keep him alive long enough. "Hector, I..." It occurred to her that he probably couldn't see Marta at all. The way the lights played in the room, and his body blocked the sunlight, he couldn't possibly see them. She needed to get him to leave. "Oh, wow, you're just in time," she said. "I was going to head back, but I was afraid it was going to get too dark."

Worse, though, if Hector figured out what was going on. Ash cleaned herself up as best she could in the dark, hoping the big lug wouldn't notice any blood. She placed a blanket over Marta, who still slept as the baby fed. They would be fine until morning, she hoped.

"I saw you walk past the quarry this morning when I was at work." Hector said when she came out.

It wouldn't have been a long walk for him if he

left from the near end of the quarry. Ash wondered why he came. She stalked past him and started on the way back toward the colony. "I came out to be alone," she said.

He didn't respond for several long breaths, but finally said, "I thought I heard someone else."

Ash stopped once she was a good distance from the cave. "Which way is it back to the colony?"

He caught up to her. Now that they were out of range of the cave, she didn't need to rush him quite so much. Hector led the way. "This way along the ridge. Then we circle around to the quarry and it's easy from there. It'll be dark by the time we get there, but that shouldn't be too bad since most of the moons are early tonight."

"Sure, but not any *good* moons."

Hector's jaw worked. "They're perfectly good moons."

"On Earth they only had one moon. You know what they called it?"

"The Moon," he said.

"The *Moon*." She hesitated, not sure what to say next. "They made a really big deal out of walking on it."

"Well, sure. They only had the one, and it was the first thing they walked on that wasn't their own planet."

Ash waved an arm at the sky. "What would they have done if they'd been in our position? I mean, we have *seven moons*. Hard to make a big deal out of walking on each one."

"We have interstellar travel already, so walking on moons is hardly even worth our time."

"See what I mean?" Ash said. "This place doesn't have any good stories to tell. All the good stuff's been done. We haven't even *named* our moons."

Hector shrugged. "Names aren't that important, really. Anyway, we'd have to all agree on a new naming system, and that's way too much work."

Ash watched the blue sun as it dipped behind the far-off storm. A green sunset glowed across the tops of dark clouds. She had forgotten her light stick back in the cave and hoped that it wouldn't get too dark before moonrise. Maybe it would be best if Marta had the light stick, anyway. "I just wish I could have seen it," she said.

"The Moon?" asked Hector. "I've seen pictures. It's round."

She took hold of the crook of Hector's elbow as they passed a treacherous length of the ridge, leaning on him a little more than she might have intended. Exhaustion rolled over her, and the long walk ahead of them dragged on. If she didn't do something she might fall asleep right there on the rocks. She kept hold of his arm as they walked, and he didn't protest. "Tell me a story, Hector," she said, hoping for at least a good distraction.

"Looking for ideas to steal for our contest?" he asked.

Her mouth dropped open in mock dismay. "You found me out!"

His chuckle was like a mountain in an earthquake. Ash fell comfortably in step next to him. She wondered who this guy was, since she'd always passed over him at social gatherings. Alone with her under the setting sun he came across as clever. Maybe he was always like that, and she never paid attention. The moons rose one by one, their twinkling brilliance reflecting the blue-white light of the setting sun.

When Hector finally spoke, his voice was a deep rumble, like his words emanated from the depths of the earth. He told her of a people who lived in great forests, their needs all met by the growth around them. They walked not on soil, but on the ancient roots of two-hundred foot plants. Wildlife teemed around, in skies and the earth. Animals and insects swarmed inside even the mightiest of trees, and the people were one with the nature around them. They never sought to master the world, because in truth they were only a part of the greater whole.

"That was lovely," she said, her voice quieter than she expected. They stood in front of her little house. "It wasn't really a *story*, but it was lovely."

His jaw tensed, but he said nothing. The pit of her stomach dropped. She's said the wrong thing and insulted the story he'd been working on for months. Letting go of his arm, she gnawed on her lower lip for the span of several long breaths.

"This was nice," she said, slipping the rebreather from her face. "Next time I'll tell you *my* story."

Before he could respond, she slipped into her cluttered little house and closed the door. She collapsed fully dressed on her bed and didn't stir until the sun came up.

CHAPTER FOUR

AFTER A SHORT AND FITFUL SLEEP, Ash dressed in cargo pants and a fresh black hoodie, keeping her coat from the previous day. She printed fresh clothes for Marta and the baby, taking her best guess at the woman's size, and giving her a variety of dark, loose styles.

She packed up her things and walked back to Marta's cave. When she arrived, she found Marta in the far corner of the room, curled in a ball on a lone blanket. The baby rested several feet away, its face turned toward the shadowed wall. Bile and sweat clung to the cave, so much that Ash choked when she breathed it, even through her rebreather.

Ash set her pack down next to Marta. It contained as much food and water as she could bring without rousing suspicion, but that wouldn't last long. She would need to bring more soon if the baby would live long enough to be integrated into the colony.

She touched the sleeping woman on the shoulder. "How are you doing?"

Marta rolled onto her back, eyes unfocused. "I'm fine," she said in a quiet voice.

Ash touched the woman's belly, feeling for—she didn't know what. It was something her mother had always done. Marta flinched from each touch.

"Are you peeing okay?" It seemed like an appropriate thing to ask.

Marta nodded without speaking.

Ash turned to the baby. She shuddered at the memory of that wretched thing. Her palms went clammy and cold at the thought of touching the strange creature. His chest rose and fell as he drew his tiny breaths. He didn't have a rebreather, and Ash made a mental note to bring one the next time she visited.

Marta rolled onto her side. The mother looked so serene compared to the previous day. The mother's words still haunted Ash. Did the Marta still regret bringing this child into the world? Wouldn't a mother do anything for her child?

She touched Marta's shoulder again. "I need to go to work today, but I'll come back as soon as I can."

Ash hurried back to her lab, where she checked on everything she had missed the previous day. She worried her samples would either die or outgrow their spaces if she didn't prep them properly before the storm.

"Olympia, how's that sample I gave you the other day?"

A broad grin broke out over Olympia's face. "Wonderful. It'll be ready for stage two tomorrow."

Ash scrolled through the history, keeping track of any anomalies that might have crept up during the incubation process and asking Traverse for clarification when the logs made no sense. One alert caught her eye. The text on the screen was hard to read, with some letters upside-down and others glitched into strange characters.

"Traverse, what is this anomalous indication?"

Traverse's spinning logo popped up in the corner. "Anomalous non-human activity has been detected in the colony."

"No kidding." Ash expanded the alert. "Was it in my lab?" she asked as she read. Her greatest fear was creating something she couldn't control, and her heart hammered at the thought of something happening while she was away.

"No," said Traverse. "The anomalous activity was outside of lab perimeter."

Ash relaxed. Nothing she did, then. Maybe one of the other labs got into something dangerous. "Well, I guess that's someone else's problem, then," Ash said. She didn't voice her real fear that Marta was the one producing anomalous activity.

Olympia said, "Did you see the message about tightened nutrient controls?"

"What?" Ash scrolled through the screen. Sure enough, her lab would be getting a smaller supply of nutrients to use in their experiments. "What is this, Traverse? How are we supposed to get any work done?"

"Reuse of materials is encouraged," said the AI.

"Thanks, jerk." Of course, they could reuse the material they already had. Those carbon, nitrogen, hydrogen, and oxygen atoms could be rebuilt thousands of times if they were careful not to lose too many of them between each printing. If that were the case, then, there would be a lot less wiggle room to steal nutrients for her ward out in the cave.

Ash chewed her lower lip for the rest of the day until a little bead of blood formed. Finally, she resolved to find another source of nutrients for Marta and the baby. She called Simon and Hector, telling them both that she really, really needed a drink, even though it wasn't their usual night to go out. Simon agreed to go, but Hector was silent. Their last moments together replayed in her mind. She remembered his kindness walking her home and how his deep storytelling voice reverberated in her chest. She also remembered how she had offended him, and her face turned deep red at the thought.

"Have I got a story for you," said Simon the moment she entered the cantina. He wore a filthy faux tweed coat, which hung like a washcloth over his wiry frame.

The place had an entirely off feel to it, like a printed house where all the corners were just off of ninety degrees. Orson stood behind the pressed fiber bar, but all the customers were different. Meeting there broke her normal routine, and it itched at her like freshly printed clothing.

Simon must have seen the reluctance on her face. "No, Ash. You can't call off the bet. You either write a story or you lose the bet. Isn't that right, Orson?"

The barkeep nodded.

"It's just we got really busy at the lab and I don't have time." Ash swiped a few plastic credits across the bar and took up two chocolate protein bars. She gestured at the door and Simon led the way out into the hallway that ran through the inside of the Commons. Ash pocketed the bars.

"You're not going to eat those?" Simon asked.

"They're for later."

He shook his head reproachfully. "Hoarding's not encouraged, you know."

She turned on him and poked him in the chest. "Don't you give me a hard time. I've got enough problems." She shook her head. "Let's eat them upstairs."

Simon changed the subject; which Ash thought was pretty wise. "So, I've been doing research."

"You're supposed to be writing a story, not a research paper. School's done, man."

He shook his head. "I know, but I remembered what you always say about the past being full of great stories. I can't really write about our life here without any reference at all to what happened to get us here."

Ash led the way through to the inner stairwell of the building. The spiral of stairs looped around a wide central atrium, and the domed ceiling above let in a brilliant display of sunlight. They walked up the stairs.

"You're really doing a historical piece? Do you need my expert expertise, because you're not going to get it." Ash really didn't think that would be his style. Ship-era stories were almost entirely happy little romance books that contained a whole lot of optimism and not much substance. Ash considered it more proof that all the good stories had been told on Earth. It was only the really old stories from Earth that had any real grit to them. "Wait. Is it a love story?"

Simon stopped, one foot on the top step. After taking several seconds to come up with something to say, he finally settled on, "Maybe."

"Dang." Ash leaned back against a segment of the glass dome.

"Anyway, did you know that seconds changed?"

Ash blinked, not understanding what he meant. "What?"

"Seconds. Minutes. Hours. All of them. Slowly, over a couple hundred years. Traverse managed it all, slowly adjusting time for the colonists so that by the time we got here everybody just knew what local days and hours and years would be like."

Ash looked out over the colony. Past the Commons rooftop lightning rod she could see all of Edge and beyond. The vantage point even let her see over the mountain and to the ocean below where the storm approached. "How different were they?" Ash had never heard of this, so she knew it wasn't in any of the fiction.

"I don't know. The days on Sky are only a couple hours longer, whatever that even means. Earth hours, I guess. That's what most of the other units are based on, so I guess our seconds are around ten percent longer than those on Earth."

Ash sat back in her chair. "Traverse changed the fabric of time itself? Just by wanting it?"

Simon nodded, then made a gesture indicating his head exploding.

"This is stressing me out, Simon." Ash leaned forward, conspiratorial gleam in her eye. "What else do you think it's changed?"

Simon stared out over the colony. "I hadn't considered that."

"It could totally be messing with us. Maybe there aren't two thousand colonists. Maybe there's no ship at all." She glanced suspiciously around. "Maybe some of the colonists are robots or clones."

"I've seen the ship pass in front of the sun." He squinted up at the sky. "I can see it right now."

"Maybe that's just a bird," Ash deadpanned.

"A ship shaped bird." Simon's laugh was infectious. "That flies around the dead planet, taunting its dead god."

Ash frowned. "It's not dead. Dead implies that it was once alive. This place has no history and never had any life. That's what makes it so boring."

Simon waggled his eyebrows. "Maybe it was alive, and Traverse just *told* us nothing lived here."

"Now you're back to telling one of your stupid future stories." Ash downed her remaining nectar. "I've been busy, Simon. I don't have time to write."

"Then mine will be the best."

"I want more time, that's all."

Simon stopped, awestruck, "Do you think chocolate flavor is the same as it is on Earth?"

Ash scowled and pointed a finger at Simon's chest. "Don't you mess with me, middle man. I will wreck you if you get me thinking all existentially about my chocolate."

Ash drew the chocolate protein bars from her cargo pocket and stared at them. Simon grinned.

"Damn," Ash said. "I hate you." She crammed them back into her pocket. "I'll eat these later," she said. The bars would help Marta out some but wouldn't be enough to last. Unfortunately, it looked like it was about as much as Ash was going to be able to take on this visit without drawing suspicion. "Have you seen Hector today?"

Simon shook his head. "I'm just a middle man, remember? Hector's all up in the big machines, all the big long day." Simon scratched the scruff on his chin. "He won't help, you know. He's going to have a story on time, too."

Tension clutched at Ash's jaw. "I should go," she said. Without waiting for a response, she slid down the long spiral handrail, letting out a whoop when she hit the bottom.

The sun set, and the sky over Edge was a wash of violet and green. She stopped to stare across the little colony, wondering how people ever came to exist in this amazing place. Had Traverse really changed the length of their days to match the new planet? It seemed likely, and hundreds of years had passed. What would it be like to return to Earth and live in their strange gravity under a strange sun? Maybe she was the alien here, but she would be even more so back home. Such was the consequence of mankind's reach for the stars.

As the sky's light dimmed, Ash's eyelids dragged. She walked to her little house, set in the side of the hill, but each step felt like slogging through thick mud. Marta had several days of food, and Ash had no doubt that the woman could survive until morning.

Ash's mother's voice came to her. A woman needed more support after the baby was born than food or drink. She needed counsel and love. Ash couldn't give love, and counsel was asking too much.

But she could be present.

After stopping at her house to raid her hidden stash of snacks, Ash set out for Marta's cave. The quarry looked like a great, dark beast had bitten a hole in the mountain. The hum of the reactor buzzed under her feet. Even after dark, the plant generated resources for the colony. When she activated her newly printed light stick, the world around disappeared, and she followed her own trail.

The way was clear now, and from time to time, she saw her own footprints—and the larger footprints of Hector—faded in the wind-torn sand. The storm loomed closer, its lightning-scarred face devouring the horizon in a yellow-black maw. She stepped with her little boots in his large ones, wishing he were there beside her. Days, Ash thought, until the storm really threatened. They had days.

How safe would Marta be in her cave? She thought of plans she might put in place to fortify the little enclosure. They could pile rocks into the entrance to block the main force of the wind, but would her cave fill with water when the rains hit? Ash did not know.

Finally, after three moons rose, Ash approached the little cave. The baby's cry, like a drowning bird, echoed through the night. It tore at her heart, that little voice. How had it grown into something so biting and strange?

He continued to cry as she approached, and with every yelp from the little beast, her heart pounded harder. What could be so wrong with so young a thing? Was he hurt or hungry? Maybe Marta was having trouble feeding after all. Breastfeeding was great when it worked but could be devastating if it failed.

Ash's pace quickened. Still, the baby cried, louder and louder. He wailed in the night with such force as to rival the oncoming storm. Ash burst into the cave without slowing a step, and saw the baby in its pile of cloth, screaming at the cave ceiling.

Screaming. Screaming. Screaming.

No mother in sight, the little baby screamed.

Ash reached out to touch the child, and her light fell across his face. For the first time, she got a good look at the hideous child. Its nose grew twisted and strange, with ridges of flesh walking up its bridge like steppes on a hill. The brow line broke in scaly skin, like fleshy horns protruding from the front of its face. Like the previous time she saw him, his mess of hair matted against its head in a greasy pile. She saw its body clearly as the coverings fell away. His umbilical cord had fallen away as it should.

Trembling, she touched the baby boy, and the screaming stopped. She picked him up, holding him carefully to her chest. He rooted at her, looking for food where he would find none. She gave him a finger to suckle, knowing that wouldn't help for long. A sharp tooth dug into her finger, and she pulled it away bloody.

"Now you see," said Marta in a ragged voice from the darkest part of the cave, "what evil I have brought into this world."

CHAPTER FIVE

"Printing an animal pseudocell is as easy as printing that of a plant or a microorganism, and once the cell's ability to reproduce a printed DNA strand is established, the process is indistinguishable from the normal processes of life," Marta said. The baby suckled at her breast, and she held him the way one holds a writhing leech. "Traverse always taught us that printing complex multi-cellular organisms strains the capabilities of the machines and is unlikely to succeed. When I was told this, I accepted it as everyone has always accepted it. Our rate of success at single celled organisms is low, and to compound that onto anything multi-celled would surely fail.

"I fell in love once." She spat the words as if they tasted bitter in her mouth. "They only allow a few children each year. My loved one was not one of the two boys in my classes. Those boys fell in love with each other and were perfectly happy for it. No, my love was a woman five years my senior. She was striking and bold. Clever in a way that people never seem to be around the labs. Her name was Bless. She worked in the bio lab, so I wanted to work in the bios, too.

"It wasn't to be, though. Traverse said they needed my skills in the medical printers, and who was I to argue? I was good at meds, with a strong head for math and a keen understanding of chemistry. I knew almost every medicine in the database, and if I couldn't print it in ten minutes, it wasn't going to get printed. The other medical techs knew I was destined for greatness. Some even talked about me one day inventing new medicines, and I did. I had a printer that was entirely offline, separate from Traverse so the AI wouldn't know what I was doing. Even then I knew to fear that machine's cold logic. I used it to combine custom molecules and test them digitally.

"Bless heard one day that Traverse was taking applications for babies, and we decided to apply together. We didn't make it, but it didn't bother us. We were happy together. That would be enough.

"Again, and again, Traverse passed us over. Lesser couples got the permission to have babies, and we never did. At first, we thought it might be because we were both women. We figured Traverse would want couples who could biologically make their own child. Bless did some research at the bio labs, though, and discovered that this wasn't the case. Many babies born on the colony or on the ship are from a gene bank. They froze inseminated eggs long ago and reintroduce those to the population on a regular basis to maintain biodiversity. The strategy allows a relatively low number of colonists to eventually produce a widely varied population, which was important to the architects of the generation ship.

"Around that time, and maybe as part of the same search, Bless discovered something else. Whole templates existed for the printing of live animal cells. The printer didn't exist that could build them yet, but if those files existed, then so, too, must the technology. Why would Traverse keep such a thing from us?

"But, there was more, and Bless, bold as she was, pursued it with bitter determination. I begged her to stop. Not only were the animal files there, but some had been genetically optimized to better survive on this planet. They would thrive in this harsh atmosphere, and their improved respiratory systems would filter out the poisonous particulates that harm us so badly if we fail to wear our rebreathers.

"So, I did what any aspiring mother would do. I started learning the intricacies of combinatorial genetic calculus. Once I got the idea into my head, there was no stopping me. Even Bless tried to calm the fire in me, but my mind was set on this one thing and I would have it. Information was more important than food to me, and I couldn't live without it. So impassioned was I, that I did not notice as my Bless wasted away from sickness. The wilting disease that eventually takes us all seized her early in her life and by the time I figured it out, it was too late. A year passed with her middling her way through, but one day she couldn't go to work, and the next, she was dead.

"If I was impassioned before, now I was obsessed. I worked myself ragged learning the tricks of genetics and mitochondrial manipulation. Gene expression was just as important as the genes themselves, and all of the knowledge of our people lay out before me in Traverse's archives. You see, there are ways to manipulate Traverse, and I found them in my research. If Bless had known this when she did her research, maybe she wouldn't have died her early death. For a while, I had my lab outside of the machine's view, and I could search for truths inside of its databanks as surely as I could manipulate the chemical makeup of the food we produce.

"So obsessed was I with a solution to the problem, that I missed my shifts at the med lab. Problems started happening, and I wasn't there to fix them. Traverse became suspicious of my anomalies, but I didn't care. I had discovered the solution to breathing on this world, and I printed the genetic strings that I needed, placing them in a single, complex cell. One single zygote, made with all of the building blocks of the perfect successor to the human condition. All scans showed that it was perfect.

"And it was alive. I implanted the zygote in myself so that it might come to term and be a person. Part of its genome descended from Bless. From that point on, I played my part in the med labs. When my coworkers accepted me back, they treated me well. They assumed I was broken by the grief of Bless's loss, but that wasn't it. The world was gray to me, and I struggled to stay focused. Several times, I printed the drug which would have ended that pregnancy, but every time I failed to take it. Doubt racked me every single day. In the end, I destroyed my hidden lab, for fear of discovery, which is why you find me here in this terrible cave with no supplies. Now, the doubt I felt makes sense to me, because the creature I've created is not human. It is a monster."

Marta looked down at the baby in her arms, a look of disgust on her face. The baby had fallen asleep, its nasal flaps flexing with each breath.

"He's not a monster," Ash said.

Marta's expression didn't change.

Ash watched the woman for a long while, wondering if there might be more to her frantic story. The madness dancing at the edge of Marta's eyes made sense to Ash—the two women struggled against the same overbearing structure of their world. She said finally, "Have you thought of a name?"

A look of tortured guilt flashed across the mother's face. "I've been so tired. I'll think of a name tonight."

"You said you had a way to manipulate Traverse. What was it?"

Marta watched Ash with flat eyes for a long time before she answered. "It's an override code," she said. "Not a full license to do whatever you like, but it lets a user delve past the AI's lies. Lets you pass through locked doors and print forbidden materials like weapons and drugs. It only works when the ship drops below the horizon, and if Traverse is not busy with some task, it will record your interactions and evaluate them later."

Ash touched the woman's arm. Her skin felt warm in the cool cave, perhaps feverish. "Rest for a while," she said. "I'll take the baby and try to keep him asleep."

Marta handed the child to Ash and curled up onto her sleeping pad. Ash listened for a long while, hoping to hear the woman's breathing slow. Eventually, Ash carried the baby outside of the cave, believing some distance might settle the mother's fears.

The baby nestled into her arms, and she held him tight as she would her own child. As she walked a path through the moonlit night, she wondered if she would ever have a child of her own, and if she did wouldn't it make sense to change the baby so that it thrived in Sky's harsh climate? She looked down at the hideous child and wondered. At what cost was this person changed? It wasn't just the ridges of bone or flaps of skin that made him hideous. Some sunken depth of her brain triggered at the wrongness of his features. His eyes were set too close, and his limbs were too long. His muscles felt toned and strong. A baby this age shouldn't be able to hold up its head, but this little boy moved and stretched in his sleep.

Predators were born into action, Ash realized. Old movies of wildlife showed the creatures up and moving almost as soon as they were born. Nature demanded that they hunt as soon as possible, but what did that say for this baby? What would that say for any society composed of creatures like this? It wouldn't be human, whatever it was. Ash felt again the revulsion to the strange creature in her arms, and at the same time her stomach twisted with guilt for that revulsion. What if this were a disfigured human child? She'd love that baby unconditionally. How was it that this felt different to her? She sat holding the child close, staring out at the sky.

Out at the oncoming storm.

CHAPTER SIX

"Traverse," Ash said the next day as she checked each of her experiments in the incubation chamber. "We're going to write a story."

"Would you like to listen to a story?" Traverse asked. The colony ship, which housed most of Traverse's computing power, had long since dipped below the horizon. Ash was beginning to detect the differences in how it behaved when it struggled to compute.

"No, Traverse. We're going to *write* a story. I haven't had time to work on it on my own, and I want to see what we can create collaboratively."

Ash stretched her muscles, still achy from sleeping on the cave floor. She had switched to brown cargo pants and a SPAM t-shirt before coming to work, but the grime of the previous day still clung to her.

Before she had left in the morning, Marta had

told her the override code. The wisest strategy was to wait until the AI was disconnected from its main processors and then get it occupied on a difficult problem. Usually that meant tricky language or processing large amounts of genetic info. Marta said she always had the computer evaluate new medicines, which took up quite a bit of modeling power. If Ash could get Traverse occupied enough, she would be able to subvert the security systems protecting the central food banks. Marta and the baby would have enough food for weeks, which is what it might take before the colony dug out from under the storm.

In theory.

"I'll give you goals," Ash said, "and you will list story elements based on those inputs."

Traverse's logo spun on her screen. "Proceed."

Ash pulled a rack of petri dishes from the incubator. The first few showed a strange contaminant. A fine dust blackened the edges of the dish. She tossed those into the recycler, not even bothering to check for viability.

"Every story I've ever really liked has started out with some big tragedy," Ash said. "All the classics like Hamlet or The Hitchhiker's Guide to the Galaxy start out with something bad happening, so let's use that as a starting point."

"Everyone dies."

"Whoa, slow down, Traverse. That's a bit much."

"Simulating catastrophic events." The logo spun for several seconds. "A megafauna theme park goes catastrophically wrong when the megafauna escapes captivity."

"I don't even know what that means, Traverse."

"Supernova."

Ash opened one of her petri dishes and found that the cell growth was strong. Under the microscope, the organism showed little variation, which made sense for an asexually reproducing single cell. She split the sample into three parts and dosed two with concentrated substrates of the atmospheric contaminants. "We want something that's really bad and promises to get much worse. If you start a story out like that, then there's motivation to keep things from getting really bad."

"What are you talking about?" Olympia said, startling Ash.

"Oh, um, nothing."

Olympia raised an eyebrow. She set up her own lab station and pulled a rack of incubating petri dishes.

Ash sighed. "I'm writing a story." She stuck a thumb out at her screen. "With that guy's help since I haven't had time to do it on my own."

Olympia's raised eyebrow strained plausibility in how high it raised.

"Slow decapitation by dull knife," Traverse said.

Ash replied, "A lot of good mysteries start with a gruesome murder, but I don't think that's where we want to go. We need a food shortage or a contamination leak or something. Maybe aliens? I don't know. Can you compute the story potential for a variety of tragic twists for me?"

Traverse said, "I do not understand the term story potential."

"Define story potential." Ash scrunched her face up trying to think of a good definition. "Like, how many predictable and unpredictable decision trees might arise with a single event as the starting point. An asteroid killing everyone wouldn't leave a lot of options, but a water contaminant that drove people insane might have plenty. We just need some options. Why don't you start by listing things that might happen in Edge?"

Traverse's logo spun for several seconds. "Definition accepted."

"Excellent. Now, what can you come up with for that?"

"A reconfiguration of ship's orbital mirrors creates a focus which rapidly raises air temperature by four hundred degrees, cooking all colonists in their homes."

"That's just great, Traverse." Ash wondered if the AI could detect her sarcasm. "You're just super creative when you're thinking of ways to kill us all."

Olympia turned her nose up at her petri dishes. "Is this stuff going to drive us insane?" she asked, holding up a contaminated dish. "Is that what's going on here?"

"Ugh," Ash said. "I'm not sure what's wrong, but I think some of our equipment got messed up. Probably something from another lab." On a whim, she brought up the alert that Traverse had shown the previous day. It still warned of an anomaly but didn't warn of anything inside the lab. "Just toss those experiments and we'll restart those after the storm."

Ash turned back to her table and processed more biological agents. For a long while, she and Olympia worked in silence. The day passed, and the shadows from the window shortened and disappeared as the blue sun made its way across the sky.

Traverse broke the silence. "A mother in a cave murders her newborn child," it said.

Ash set down her scalpel, forcing herself not to react with the panic that welled up in her chest. "What did you say?"

"A mother murdering her child is a tragic act which has significant story potential. Many stories have handled this over the years, from redemption to prosecution. It might be a murder mystery or a tale of insanity-causing contamination. It is possibly a medical mystery or horror."

"You can do better. Keep working on it," Ash said, failing to keep her voice from shaking. When she looked up she saw Olympia's eyes on her. "I need to leave early," she said.

Olympia went back to her work. After putting away her tools and her remaining petri dishes, Ash hurried across town. The ship still flew below the horizon, and Traverse still worked on her story ideas. Now was her best time to get food enough for Marta. Even though it was broad daylight, she would need to load up everything she could carry and get out to the cave fast. Marta's strange mood from the previous day worried her, and Traverse had struck the core of that worry right in the heart.

She was so lost in her thoughts as she crossed town, that she ran smack into Hector as she rounded a corner. Her smaller frame bounced off his, and she tumbled to the ground.

"Sorry!" He knelt down to help her.

She grasped his arm and pulled herself up. In a split-second decision, she dragged him along with her toward the Commons. "Come on," she said. "I need your help."

"Ash, wait," he said.

She didn't wait, and he followed.

The colony stored food supplies among various buildings, the resource being too valuable to keep in one place. Places like the labs always had a week or two's worth of general supplies, and feedstock enough to print a variety of foods. The bulk of the long-term feedstock supply sat in the center of the Commons where many colonists would wait out the storm. It was like a big festival, if festivals were when everyone cowered from a devastating common threat.

She led Hector past the cantina to the stairwell.

Up above, sunlight refracted through the glass roof of the Common's large central dome. Instead of circling up the stairs, she ducked down to the service entrance to the automated storage vault. The reinforced door had a console built into it.

"Traverse," she said. Then she spoke in clear tones a long string of numbers that made up the override code. "Override locks, I need to enter."

"Ash, wait. What are you doing?" Hector said, panting from trying to keep up with her.

"I'll explain once we're done." Ash turned to Hector and looked him straight in the eyes. "Do you trust me?"

He hesitated.

"Good. And I trust you, too. This is important, and we need to hurry."

The door clicked, then opened. She rushed into the room, ready to fill her pack with enough feedstock to last a woman and her baby several weeks. The dense feedstock material was a stable amalgamation of all the molecules human beings needed for survival, and any of the colony's printers could turn that material into food. Even Marta's med printer could make a decent bread or meat substitute. It could even simulate vegetables, though now that Ash thought about it, she really didn't know how close any of the simulations were. After all, she'd never really eaten a real spear of broccoli or a real steak. They might not even be the right color.

With enough feedstock, Marta wouldn't just be

able to survive, she could make herself the comfort foods she needed to get out of whatever funk she'd descended into. That madness at the edge of the mother's eyes still haunted Ash, and she longed to get out there to the woman as soon as possible.

Ash stopped. Traverse had said they had food enough for an entire year. Water was plenty, and stores were stable. The AI had shown her the manifest for each building. Every bit of food was accounted for and there was plenty. Plenty!

The store room was empty.

"Ash," Hector said slowly, his quiet voice echoing in the large room. "That cave I met you at the other day…"

"Yeah?" Ash's voice sounded small and weak in her own ears.

"Marta needs your help." An edge of panic crept into Hector's voice. "She needs your help right away."

CHAPTER SEVEN

"You were spying on me?" Ash demanded, furious. They descended a set of hewn steps into a garage bunker near the quarry.

"They tell us to keep an eye out for subversives."

"They?"

Hector scratched his head. "Traverse does. It was part of the training before we came down. They had lots of horror stories about how subversives can divert colony resources and cause a collapse by, I don't know, stealing from the central reserve?"

"I'm starting to think I shouldn't have trusted you, Hector."

"You shouldn't have trusted me."

"I'm *this* close to not trusting you." She wasn't.

They crossed a long concrete slab, monstrous machines towering above them on each side. It was all Ash could do to keep from craning her neck at them. "Wait," she said. "You think I'm *subversive*?"

"It seemed likely."

Ash seethed. She had started liking Hector, and he was trying to spy on her. She clenched her jaw tight.

"I went back to the cave the day after I saw you there," Hector said. "Marta's parents were friends with mine when I was a kid." He loosened the tie downs on one of the spider-like construction walkers. It was one of the smaller vehicles, but also one of the more mobile. "She was always a little strange, but as a kid I was in her borough on ship. I thought she was fantastic."

"Are you sure we can take this?" Ash asked despite herself. She hugged her thin coat against the cold as the temperature dropped from an easterly breeze. "Won't that be too subversive?"

"Brilliant," Hector said. "Marta was always brilliant, but she had trouble understanding people sometimes." He loosened the last strap and opened the cabin door, waving Ash inside.

The spider walker stood twice as tall as Hector; its brutal design a testament to the natural shapes of Earth spiders. Its front legs jutted forward, tipped with mining cutters. The back six legs allowed the thing to traverse all manner of terrain, even the broken land of the quarry. The cabin where the driver sat was in the center where the legs connected, and behind it sat a bulging storage container.

Hector climbed in, settling himself comfortably

into the single seat. Ash looked at him questioningly.

"You could ride in the back," he said.

"I'm not your cargo, Hector." Ash climbed into the cabin, defiantly careless with her knees and elbows, and sat all the way to one side with her legs resting uncomfortably next to Hector's. With her crammed off to the side, Hector was able to reach most of the controls. He squeezed the door shut and powered up the console. He let his rebreather drop from his face, and Ash followed suit. The inside of the cabin had its own filtration.

He reached her direction, then hesitated. "Can you?"

Ash looked down. She was sitting on a slider that he clearly wanted to move. She took hold of it and slid the bar up. As she did, the spider's six walking legs flexed, raising the cabin several feet. Hector nudged the controls forward, and the spider walked out of the open-faced garage and into the quarry.

Hector said. "When I followed you the other day, I could have sworn there was something going on that you weren't telling me."

Ash's brow furrowed. "You could have asked."

"You're... a little intimidating."

She punched him on his big, meaty shoulder. "I'm not."

"Well, you clearly didn't want to tell me anything."

Ash made a "Well, duh," gesture. Her butt brushed the slider and the whole spider lurched.

"Yeah, yeah, I know." In his defense, he did sound genuinely sorry. "But it bugged me, and Traverse is really strict about how we need to follow up if we see something wrong."

Ash thought about the empty warehouse. Of all the wrong things she'd ever seen, that was the worst. The implications for not only the survival of the colony, but also for the lies that Traverse had told them. Why would the AI lie?

Hector continued, "When I got there, I saw Marta and her kid. She seemed fine at first, but I don't know. Something bothered her."

"Did you get a good look at the baby?"

"Yeah. He looks like a little alien. Like something's wrong with him." Hector maneuvered the spider walker down through the quarry, the ride surprisingly smooth, even when they mounted enormous boulders. "She told me her baby would be feared."

"He might be."

"Sure," Hector said. "People can get over that, though. I mean, it's just a kid."

The spider rounded a corner of the quarry, and Ash looked out into the storm-blackened sky. Yellow slashes of lightning played across the western sky, and the far-off rumble of thunder rolled over the open waters and up the mountain. She took hold of

Hector's big hand, her eyes wide. "It's getting close," she said, breathless.

Hector cranked the controls and the spider lurched faster. "We have to get them back to the colony before the storm hits."

"We can't," Ash said. "Traverse will kill him."

The spider rumbled forward, dropping several feet. Ash tumbled around in the cabin like a tossed doll, landing in Hector's lap. It was more comfortable than sitting on the controls, so she stayed there.

Hector's face turned red, but he didn't comment on her change in position. "I'm not buying it. Traverse takes care of colonists. How could he even kill anyone?"

"How?" Ash scrambled to find something to grip so she wouldn't bruise herself on the cabin walls. It didn't work. "There are a thousand ways Traverse could kill people. Poison, industrial accidents, cutting laser malfunction. Pretty much anything. It's a pretty robust AI, you know."

Hector shook his head. "It doesn't do that, though. When have you heard of anyone on the colony ever dying, except for..."

"Atmospheric toxicity." Ash completed his thought. "Or at least, something similar to it."

"It wouldn't do that," Hector said, not sounding as convinced this time.

The spider trundled along the path for a time. It didn't move much faster than a jog, but Ash never would have been able to manage a jog across those rocks. The spider could get them to the cave faster, but she wondered what they might find when they got there. Plus, she had no food to bring the new mother, so how much was she really helping?

"What made you decide she needed my help right away?" Ash asked after a time.

"I went down there again today, just to check on her." Hector kept his eyes focused on the rocks outside. "She seemed even more agitated than yesterday. I told her things would work out, but she wouldn't listen to reason. She holds that baby like it might explode."

"Babies do that sometimes."

"Sure, but not the way I was thinking." He flashed a smile, which faded quickly. "She isn't feeding it like she should, I don't think. Not that I'm an expert. Anyway, I told her I'd print her some formula, you know, as a backup."

"Seems reasonable."

"That set her off, shouting at me, and telling me she was mother enough for her baby. It's like she wants to be some ideal mother but also she hates her kid." He shook his head. "I don't know. Anyway, eventually, she dozed off, so I powered up her med printer to make the formula, but when I did that I saw her most recent work."

Ash's hands went cold. She knew what Hector was going to say before he said it.

"She was working on developing an arsenic derivative, Ash. I don't know my meds all that much, but the simulations she was running had to do with giving a baby a quick, painless death. An adult, too."

"Did you wreck her machine?"

"No." Hector's expression grew grim. "If her machine broke, she'd probably find a cliff to hop off of. Instead, I overrode the machine and told it to print formula instead. It looked like it'd take a while anyway, but I threw in some loops to her program that would delay a few more hours. I'm not much of a programmer, so that was the best I could come up with."

Ash placed a hand over his. "You did good, Hector," she said. He smiled, and her heart started beating double fast.

She recognized the area around the cave and motioned for Hector to stop. Before he had a chance to react, she hit the slider, dropped the spider to the ground, and extracted herself from the cabin. Soon as the door opened, the cold air knocked the breath from her lungs. Wind whipped through the space in front of the cave entrance in a vicious circle. Slapping her rebreather to her face, she hurried for the cave. The baby's howls carried through the swirling winds.

The baby screamed, which meant it lived. Relief and fear washed through her at once because the scream wasn't the same as the hungry yelp she had heard before. This scream was a hoarse rasp of a scream—an exhausted scream of a child desperate for connection that just wasn't there.

Two moons hung shrouded in the sky, their light hooded by dust kicked up in front of the storm. Ash thumbed her light stick on, but the cave entrance still yawned like a black maw. The baby's scream echoed into the night, and Ash shouted for Marta.

Ash stopped at the entrance, heart pounding in her chest. Something felt strange, and her nerves played tricks with the flickering lightning at her back. She stepped into the cave, pulling her rebreather from her face. "Marta?" she said, her voice lost in the baby's screams. "Marta!"

When there was no response, she continued into the cave, going for the place she knew the baby slept. The way the screams echoed it seemed like the creature was everywhere, his voice crushing its way into her skull. How wretched that thing must be down here in the cave? Cold seeped into her bones.

She stepped over the debris of a shattered printer. Filthy cloths and ruined food covered the cave floor, and Ash made her way through the broken contents of medical supplies. The baby's nest, where she had seen it sleep, lay empty and scattered.

Hector's silhouette eclipsed the cave entrance. "Ash, where are you?" he asked.

"Here," she said. "Looking for the baby."

Ash swept a focused beam across the cave, shocked by the destruction she found. Her light caught movement: Marta's face bound in fury. In the stunned second it took to return to that spot, the mother fled. The baby screamed its ragged, horrifying scream. The noise grated on Ash's spine and pierced deep into her skull. No baby ever screamed like that when her mother had cared for the newborns of their borough on the ship. Ash had trouble imagining anything human making that terrible sound.

Marta's voice echoed through the cave. "I made a mistake bringing this thing to life," she said. "Now we'll all pay for my sins if I don't send this monster back to hell."

Ash swung her light toward the voice, finally finding the mother. Marta stood, torn clothes draped from her body. Her hair hung in ragged lumps, and her mottled skin shone with oil and filth. In one arm she held her monstrous offspring, and in the other a sharp fragment of her printer. She held the jagged edge up to the baby's throat, but the mother's hands shook and went no further.

"Marta, please," Ash said. "We can make things better. This can work." As she spoke she realized the smooth fabrication of her lies. They couldn't make it work. She saw no real way forward that involved the survival of the baby. Maybe her words were the manifestation of some innate optimism, but more likely they were pure lies. Yet, she couldn't stop telling her story. "Hand me the baby, Marta. I'll bring him to safety, and we can figure out how to change Traverse's mind."

"You don't understand," Marta said. "For this child to live, another colonist must die—someone who would not otherwise be dead. Murder will be this child's first influence, and murder will be his legacy."

"Our borough went over population on the ship once a long time ago," Ash said, "when my mother was in charge of the births. Our cap was a thousand people, but they skirted that limit and one day a woman gave birth to triplets. That threw off the schedule, and the next woman to give birth had to convince Traverse to allow the population to exceed a thousand. Someone got sent off early to retirement, and the little baby girl lived." Ash took a step closer, arms held wide. "That was me. My mother kept me, and my father went off early to the retirement borough."

Marta's expression did not change. "This child has no father."

"Hector is here," Ash said. "He'll help."

Marta's makeshift blade backed an inch from the screaming baby. "What could he possibly do?" Marta said.

Hector approached Marta from the side, but Ash dared not look his direction. Marta didn't hear his approach because of the screams. "He's here to help you. To help *us*. We're all on the same team here, and I understand if you need a break." Ash kept her voice as steady as possible, but the need to speak over the rushing wind and screaming baby made her feel like she shouted every word in mad fury. "Hand me the baby, Marta. I'll take care of everything."

Marta took a step back, holding the baby close. Hector froze, because her new vantage point might reveal his location. Ash turned her light so that Marta would be blind to his approach, but still, he didn't move.

"You won't do anything," Marta spat. "You won't do what needs to be done. The monster needs to be destroyed, or he'll kill all of us. He's the end of humanity, and with one slash I can save us all." Fresh tears rolled freely down her cheeks.

"But you can't, can you?" Ash said. "A mother can't kill her own child. He's not a monster, Marta. He's your son. If you really were going to kill him, you would have already. So, hand me the baby." She stepped closer, arms outstretched. "Please, Marta."

Marta tensed, grimace on her face, and drew back the blade, tensed for a fatal strike.

Hector caught her arm. Marta's scream curdled blood worse than her son's. She spun on Hector and lashed out with a kick at his knee. He shouted, more in surprise than pain. Ash lunged, grabbing for the baby.

Marta shoved the baby at Ash. Ash caught the child and stumbled back. Marta grabbed her makeshift blade with her now-free hand. She stabbed Hector. He didn't cry out, but Ash saw a flash of deep red before the light stick hit stone and shattered.

Ash stumbled deeper into the cave. The baby's cry drowned out all other sounds. She hunched her body around the little creature, holding it close to her chest, knowing the blow could come at any moment. A single stab to her back or a slash across her neck. She imagined a thousand ways her blood could spill on the floor if Marta wanted to kill her there in the dark.

The baby's cries sputtered and stopped. The wind howled through the cave, empty as the most penetrating silence Ash had ever heard.

It took effort to break the silence. "Hector?"

Her eyes adjusted to the darkness, picking out shadows in the cold depths of stone. She crawled over to the most conspicuous shape and found the big man. His belly was a mess of warm blood.

"Hector," she said, probing his body. He breathed, but only softly. When she touched his side, he winced, and his breathing hitched.

She needed light, but what had happened to the lights she had given Marta? Maybe one would still function if she could find it. Ash crept along the floor, searching the filthy debris. She found equipment and dirty cloths, but no lights.

Hector moaned.

Ash ventured closer to the mouth of the cave where flashes of lightning brought an irregular strobe of visibility. There, she scanned by focusing her eyes and waiting for each yellow pulse of light. She found the lamp she had originally brought to Marta. Seizing it in two hands, she twisted to turn it on.

Hector sat with his back against the wall. He squinted at her, blinded by her light, but he lived. A tightness released in her chest when she saw him there among the garbage. Blood covered his chest and arms, but he lived. Oh, he lived.

Marta was nowhere to be seen.

CHAPTER EIGHT

HECTOR MOANED like a dying water buffalo when Ash cinched the makeshift bandage into place, but the bandage held. The worst of his wounds split the flesh an inch under his ribcage, and the skin puckered in a way that made Ash's stomach roil.

"If she'd had a real weapon I'd be dead," Hector said, almost to himself.

Ash shot him a sideways smile. She picked up a piece of Marta's med printer, turning it over in the dim light. They would need to print more formula for the baby before long. The stuff Hector had printed earlier was almost all wasted, but Ash found a few containers of it near the cave entrance.

"At least you'll get a good story from this," she said.

"Yeah, the story of how a woman half my size kicked my ass."

Ash gestured with a flourish. "Because you were

too chivalrous to strike back, and she took advantage of your gentle nature."

"I was trying to knock her out in one hit."

"So, you've learned your lesson?"

"Don't hit girls?"

Ash shadow boxed. "Use lots of little punches."

Hector laughed, but the movement jostled his wounds and he ended up alternating between laughter and tears.

"We have to find her," Ash said.

Hector's laughter stopped. "I don't know, Ash..."

"The storm's coming. She won't survive outside of the colony, especially without this cave for protection."

"Ash, *we* won't survive outside of the colony." Hector heaved his body up, propping himself into a seated position against the wall. "And the baby won't, either. She probably ran back to town, and that's where we should go, too."

"Are you stable?" Ash asked as she picked up another piece of the printer and fitted it. Most of the parts weren't broken so much as forcibly disassembled. There was still a chance they had enough parts for a working device.

"Yeah, I'm fine," Hector said, wincing.

"We can modify the spider to carry you and the baby in the back compartment, and I'll drive."

Hector sputtered. "You'll what?"

"I watched you drive. It's not so hard."

"So, I'll be your cargo?"

A big grin crossed her face. She slapped Hector on the shoulder. "You'll have company."

Hector's expression remained skeptical, but there really wasn't another way. With Ash's help, he got to his feet. Once standing, he was able to hobble out to where the spider sat. The wind swirled around the cave entrance, pulling his hair up at all angles and threatening to topple him. He worked the controls on the back of the walker, opening the modular abdomen so he could climb in.

Ash found another piece of the printer: the control module. She powered it up, verified that it acknowledged its motley assortment of parts, then stowed it in the back of the spider along with the remains of their feedstock. Maybe if Hector had time, he could work the thing and produce something like food.

Ash left the baby sleeping in a pile of blankets while she helped Hector into the spider. Every second away from the little guy sent nervous jitters down her spine. She almost felt like a real parent. When Ash was young, her mother always kept her close. She never appreciated it until the day she boarded the shuttle for Edge. Her mother became a phantom limb that she always expected to be there and only produced agony in its absence. She always resented her mother for that, but now taking care of the baby made her miss her mother with renewed pain.

The bulbous abdomen compartment on the

back of the spider easily held Hector. He slumped backward into the space and sweat beaded on his brow. Ash worried he might pass out.

She scooped the baby up, nest and all, and placed him in the crook of Hector's arm.

Hector looked with trepidation down at the little creature. "He's uglier than most," he said, "but it's a cute kind of ugly."

Ash wrinkled her nose. "I suppose."

"Hey, all babies are ugly unless you're the parents. You know that, right?"

Ash closed the compartment on them, protecting them from the wind.

The spider walker was a lot harder to drive than she thought. She nudged a lever gently, hoping to ease into movement. Nothing happened. She pushed harder, and the spider lurched to one side. Its belly ground against the gravelly earth.

"Okay," she said. "Okay."

Hector's muffled voice came through the cabin wall, barely audible over the rushing wind. "You have to raise the body."

"Shush," she called back. "You'll wake the baby."

Ash touched the slider and raised the body. When she nudged the lever, the spider started its smooth walk, easing along the trail, only it spun clockwise as it walked. It moved the right direction but rotated once every twenty seconds. She scowled at the controls, adjusted a few things, and made it much, much worse.

"Work the feet," Hector called.

Feet. Of course. Ash slipped her feet into the boot-like controls. A prickling sensation crawled up her legs. Vibrations of a hard, unyielding earth tapped back with every step. She pitched her feet to the left, and the spider stopped spinning. It took some time to grow accustomed to controlling so many of her own limbs, and she still didn't fully understand how that mapped to the eight limbs of the spider. When Hector drove, it felt like the machine did everything, but now she understood that really it was the human driver in control.

She peered through the window at the dark rocks, slashing the spider's headlights from side to side. There! A streak of blood marred a stone farther down the path. It led away from the colony and circled forward along the side of the mountain.

Ash hesitated. Hector seemed stable, and she was certain Marta wouldn't survive the storm. She turned to follow the woman's bloody trail. So much for heading back to town.

Another mark marred the path, then another. Scrambled footprints showed the places where Marta had stumbled and fallen. The bloody marks lessened after a time, since Marta was not bleeding. Ash wondered at how much blood Hector had lost— if maybe he was exaggerating how well he could handle the trip. He hadn't wanted to go, after all.

They had only gone for a half hour, however, before they saw a building. At first, Ash thought they had turned around and returned to the colony, but the building didn't seem right. The color was off, and even in the oddly tinted headlights, Ash could see that the design was slightly different, with cantilevered roofs and rough-textured fiber walls.

"Hector?" she said, hopefully loud enough that her passenger would hear. "You have to see this."

The big man did not respond, so she kept moving forward. They passed another building, then another. Cold wind whistled against the spider's carapace. Ash shivered, sensing a sudden drop in temperature outside. The storm grew closer, but she couldn't leave this mystery now. If anything, they could weather the storm in one of these buildings.

Ash maneuvered the walker up over a rise and stopped. The colony lay out before her; silent, still buildings stood as dark shadows against the strobe lightning. They sat cold and lifeless, and if any colonists resided here, they stayed hidden.

But how could anyone be living here? So close to the other colony, somebody would have noticed. Wouldn't they? Nobody hiked this way often, she was sure, but scouts frequently searched the terrain by drone and sometimes in vehicles. This place would have shown up on the video feed.

Traverse would know of the other colony since it

was visible from space. The AI *must* have kept it a secret, but why?

"I know this place," Ash muttered to herself. The layout of the town mimicked exactly the layout of Edge. She turned her spider and spied the place her lab would be. There, indeed, sat a building very much like her own.

Outside of the lab, she disconnected herself from the spider's controls and climbed out. She opened the back, relieved to see Hector still snuggled comfortably with the baby. She gestured for him to climb out.

Hector handed her the sleeping baby and extracted himself as gingerly as he could. When his feet hit the ground he said, "What's the plan?" Then he saw the buildings. His jaw did a few false starts before he said, "This isn't home, is it?"

Ash shook her head. "Another colony, I think."

Hector reached out to touch the building, as if he were having trouble believing its existence. "It feels different."

"Rougher," Ash said. "I wonder if it's an improvement on the design or an earlier model?"

"The coarser material would be easier to make quickly."

Ash approached the door with the odd sense of trespassing on someone else's sacred space. Her lab always meant so much to her, and even though she shared it with other techs and scientists, it felt more like home than her actual house. Everything she cared about lived in the incubating chambers of her section of the lab. What would she find here? She drew a deep breath and pushed the door open.

Lights came on with a flicker, illuminating a layout similar to her own lab, but, again, different in subtle ways. The main hall was longer, and thin dividers segmented some of the lab benches. The place where she and Olympia worked was nicely redesigned, she thought, with a little more space to spread out equipment. If Ash didn't have such a sentimental attachment to her own lab space, she might envy this setup.

"Is this your lab?" Hector asked. He had never been to her lab at their colony. As a large machine specialist, he had little use for bio labs. "Everything's shiny and new."

It was true. Nothing showed years of use like her lab. The tabletops were polished fiber, and the floors didn't have even a single scuff mark. All of the equipment had a crisp, unused look like freshly cut crystal. The lab even smelled of the warm amber glow of freshly printed materials. Ash touched the printer console at her workspace and was surprised when the screen came alive. An odd variation of Traverse's logo spun silently.

She opened her mouth to ask Traverse where they were but thought of a better question. "Traverse, are you connected to the ship right now?"

"No," Traverse responded. "Ship connection is expected in nine hours."

Nine hours. That gave her some time to figure out what was going on. "Traverse," she said. "I'm going to need systems access." She spouted the string of numbers Marta had told her, hoping that this instance of Traverse unlocked with the same key.

"Systems access granted," said the machine. "How can I help you."

Now, she could be reasonably certain of its answers. "Traverse, how long has this colony been here?"

"This colony construction started one hundred twenty-one days ago."

Hector leaned forward. "They built this that fast? Who built this?"

"This colony was constructed using automated systems."

The big man swayed on his feet. "Why build a second colony?"

Traverse's logo spun around several times before answering. "Automated construction drones worked quickly to build the replacement colony as soon as colony collapse was deemed inevitable."

Ash tugged at Hector's sleeve and whispered to him. "Inevitable? What happened a hundred and twenty-one days ago to make it think collapse would be inevitable?"

Hector shrugged.

"Traverse, when are we scheduled to move to this new colony?"

Traverse took even longer to consider this question. "No moves are scheduled for current colonists."

Did that mean they were training new colonists? Ash didn't voice the question. She'd endured long years of training before being sent down to the colony. She hadn't realized that Traverse was training another batch so soon. Her mother would have mentioned it at some point if she had known, but information didn't travel freely between boroughs. She might not have known.

Then an idea struck her. "Traverse," she said, "will there be two colonies?"

"No."

"Will the existing colonists be sent back to the ship?"

"No."

Hector said, "What does that mean? Ash, what does that mean?"

"It means Traverse detected something that will destroy Edge," she said. "And it's going to start a new colony." The baby stirred in her arms but didn't wake.

"Edge's food, then," Hector said. "It must be here. It took fifty years for the ship's preliminary probes to build our colony and prep our landing site. They must have stolen resources from Edge to make this place."

"And they've learned some, too." Ash swept across the screen to look at the logged messages.

This machine showed no warnings. "Traverse learned something, and its programming decided that we're expendable. Or contaminated, even. Something in its programming decided that we're so bad off that we're doomed." She ran a hand across the pristine lab bench and thought of the contaminated incubator back at her own lab.

Hector sat heavily on a stool, catching his balance with one hand. His skin was pale and damp, and each breath he drew sounded like a hard-fought battle.

"Traverse," Ash said, "what is the source of the contamination? Why is Edge condemned?"

The logo spun in silence.

Ash said, "It must not have a connection to the other colony, so the query doesn't work. It'll get a connection to the ship soon enough, but until then, we won't know what the problem is."

"But, when that connection comes back, won't the other colony learn about us visiting this one?"

Ash ran her fingers through her hair. "We have to find Marta."

"Ash, think about it. What do they do when contamination threatens to spill into neighboring cultures in your bio lab?" Hector said.

"She must be in the colony somewhere."

"There's not time." He swayed on his stool, clutching the edge of the lab bench.

Ash ignored him, turning to the screen. "Traverse, is Marta somewhere in this colony?"

The baby squirmed in her arms. It opened its eyes and looked up at her. She couldn't figure out why she ever feared this little creature. The baby certainly wasn't human, but did that make it such a terrible thing? Someday his descendants might populate this planet. It only needed the chance to survive and grow. He rooted around, searching for food. Ash stretched out a hand, and Hector placed the first of their formula pouches into it. The baby took to it quickly and devoured the nutrient-rich food.

Traverse brought up a map of the new colony, showing them as three green dots in the bio lab building. One dot blinked near the Commons.

"Ash." Hector said, a rumble of warning entering his voice. He leaned heavily on the table.

"There," Ash said, "We can swing by there, pick her up, and—"

Hector slipped from his stool, crashing to the hard floor, unconscious.

CHAPTER NINE

HECTOR CAME AWAKE in a blaze of fury when Ash
stuck the freshly printed smelling salts under his
nose. The big man lay exactly where he fell, since
she couldn't possibly move him. A short distance
away, the baby lay with wide eyes taking in everything around.

"Settle down," Ash said in the calmest voice she
could manage. "You'll rip your bandages again."

His wild eyes focused on her, seeming to
struggle to recognize her. Hector's shoulders
slumped, and he relaxed. "What's going on?"

"I redid your bandages as best I could, and
managed to get some synthetic blood into you," said
Ash. "You were still bleeding quite a bit, and probably shouldn't move for a couple days."

Hector prodded at the neatly bound bandages
on his chest. He rubbed his arm where a new
bandage marked the spot she had used to inject the

blood. The shredded remains of the old blood-soaked bandages decorated the printer console. "How long has it been?"

"We need to leave. An hour ago."

His eyes focused on something far away for a few seconds. "Marta," he said.

"You were right. We need to leave her for now. She'll be fine as long as she's in one of these buildings during the storm. What we need to do right now is get home and figure out why Traverse thinks the colony is doomed."

Hector's throat made a dry click when he swallowed. Ash handed him a pouch of nutrient liquid, and he drank in slow sips. "How long have I been out?"

"Long enough." She offered him an arm and helped him to his feet. He leaned on her hard, and she wondered if he would be able to stand on his own at all. "Let's get you into the walker."

"The storm."

"It's getting nasty, but not on us in full force yet."

Outside, sleet pelted them in furious waves. Ash led the big man to the spider and opened the back. He tried to step in, but his hand slipped. He nearly crushed her as they both toppled to the icy mud. Ash lay on the ground staring up as yellow lightning danced across the sky. Icy cold seeped through her clothes, past her skin, and deep down into her bones.

"Sorry," Hector said.

Ash's body started to shake, and she thought maybe the driving cold made her shiver. When the corners of her mouth started turning up, she realized that she was laughing. She laughed, loud and strong at the raging storm above. When she turned to Hector, she saw, at first, the open jaw of a man who couldn't believe the insanity of the person who controlled whether he lived or died.

Then, Hector started to laugh, too. Cold mud ran off of them in rivulets, and sleet pelted their faces. They laughed at the lightning sky and the raging preliminaries of the dangerous storm. When they'd laughed their breaths away, they drew deep the frigid air of the hostile planet.

And they laughed some more.

Ash, finally, stood and helped Hector into the abdomen. She closed him in while she got the baby bundled into a waterproof wrap back in the building. He nuzzled close to her, his little body generating an amazing amount of heat. She handed him to Hector, and the big man cuddled the baby. Their eyes met and heat rose in her that threatened to burn away the freezing rain.

"The little guy likes you," Ash said.

"I've got the food."

Ash climbed into the cabin, hoping that the machine wouldn't fail if she got the console wet. It had been designed to withstand the elements, however, and would likely be fine. She dropped her feet into the boot harness, slid the spider's body up, and moved.

Ten minutes later, the storm hit hard. Sheets of sleet gave way to a cacophony of hail and rain. Wind threatened her spider walker, shunting it aside. Powerful legs struggled against the barrage, and Ash's own legs felt the brunt of their struggle. She twisted the spider around, facing it into the straight-line winds as best she could. The spider crept sideways with her driving nearly blind in the powerful storm.

She couldn't stop. Not now. They would never survive the storm, and she felt foolish for bringing Hector and the baby, risking their lives. No matter that the two likely wouldn't have survived on their own in the lab.

With a renewed determination, Ash pushed the spider forward. She slid the slider down three quarters of the way, and the spider's body lowered enough that wind no longer swept underneath. She kept the spider close against the cliff wall, as far from downslopes as she could manage and out of the wind.

As much as anything could be out of the wind.

Lightning lit the skies and scorched the land. Sharp crackles and vicious thunder shattered the night. Her reflection flashed in the spider's glass, maddened and lit only by the crack-slash strobe of the sky's fury. The storm was the fiercest punishment of a hostile planet. It was the crushing power of the world's dead god.

No, not dead, she reminded herself. Something needed to be alive first in order to be dead. This god never lived. It never brought life to this planet, and so the planet was nothing more than potential. It was a skeleton waiting to be suffused with flesh. A made thing, ever waiting for that one life-giving breath of its creator.

A breath that Ash might one day give it.

She laughed as she drove the spider onward. Cold, dripping wet, and mad. All these things, but not dead. Not this day.

Lightning arced across the front of the spider, blinding her. The crash rang in her ears and by instinct she shied from the front of the vehicle. When she opened her eyes, she saw the stony ridge to their left crumbling from impact or rain.

She tried to dance free, but with the spider sitting so low it couldn't move sideways quickly. Stones tumbled down a dozen feet to strike the left legs, pinning two of them. Something to that side shifted, and the whole spider lurched. No matter how much she cranked the controls, the spider wouldn't move.

When her hearing returned, she heard the baby crying.

"Hector, are you all right back there?" she called.

"We're fine." His voice was barely audible over the rushing storm. "Just a little upset."

"The spider is stuck." Ash tried again to dislodge the vehicle. It wouldn't come. "I need to go out there."

"I'll go," Hector said.

"No!" Ash searched the cabin for anything that might help. She found a small tool kit and stuffed it in her spacious cargo pocket. No wonder people on Earth loved this kind of pants so much. "I'll go. You take care of the baby."

Soon as the door was open a crack, the wind tore it open all the way. Cold rain swirled around the cabin, soaking anything that wasn't already damp and cold. Ash stuck her head out, trying to see what held them back. In all the rain and sleet and mud, she couldn't see anything.

She jumped out, holding tight to the spider's frame. Wind grasped at her clothes as she crawled down to the legs.

One battered leg hung useless from the carapace, but another had twisted as a boulder several feet in diameter shifted onto it. Pinned as it was, it couldn't move, and she couldn't get it free. Without at least two legs on that side, she didn't think it could walk at all. She wondered if one of the two arms could function as a leg for movement, but she doubted it.

Ash swore and took hold of the pinned leg. Rifling through the toolkit, she found a specialized tool for detaching leg hardware. The twisting pressure on it from the boulder made work difficult, and her fingers grew numb from cold. After several minutes of futile effort, she gave up and started work on the dangling leg. That one had serious structural damage, but the bolts where it attached to the main body still functioned. She detached the leg with no trouble.

She tried again to sever the pinned leg. It wouldn't budge. Hail the size of her precious penny fell, and she ducked under the spider for protection.

While huddled under the vehicle, she wondered if this might be her tragic twist. It certainly felt like one. Funny how Traverse never came up with "died by lightning strike while huddled under a broken spider while the man she might be falling for hid inside with a baby that wasn't hers." It wasn't a very good start of a story, but it made a pretty solid end.

"How's it going in there?" she asked through the underside of the spider's abdomen.

"Fine," came the response. The baby screamed. "Could be better."

Three spider legs on one side and one on the other did her little good, but from under the body they looked interchangeable. When the hail subsided, Ash detached the middle leg from the right side and plugged it into the front left position. She climbed into the cabin, which now had half a foot of water on the floor. The door wouldn't close, with the wind whipping at it at such an angle, so she left it.

Feet in the boots again, Ash worked the controls slowly, keeping her head out the door so she could see. With slow, strong pressure at just the right angle, she eased the pinned leg up. Ever so slowly, the metal limb scraped along the bottom of the boulder. When it stopped moving, she reset her legs, adjusted her height, and pulled again.

It came free, and the spider stumbled several feet the other direction before she regained control. She rotated the spider so that the wind hit it at a different angle and closed the door.

She sat for several deep, ragged breaths, taking in the deafening white noise of her enclosed space. It took her a moment, but she realized that the baby had stopped crying, and thanked Hector silently for that one blessing.

The spider no longer walked smoothly. It lurched and hobbled, making its way clumsily forward. She estimated that the quarry would be on her left, but the fierce storm outside prevented any attempts at verifying that hunch. She worked the walker forward, keeping to level ground as well as she could. When she saw the first building of the colony, she let out a long, shivering breath. They had made it to safety, but she wasn't done yet. She needed to get to the Commons, where the cantina and most of the supplies were. It was only another two hundred feet, but a wall of hail blocked their way. The noise of it hitting the spider's shell sounded like the earth itself cracking apart. She nudged the controls forward.

The spider didn't move.

Ash slammed a fist on the console. Nothing. The boot controls became lead on her feet, water sloshing as she jerked them around.

"It's not working!" she shouted, hoping Hector could hear. When he didn't respond, she pounded on the controls again, and wrenched her feet from the dead controls.

The hail subsided, leaving behind it an eerily gentle rain. Visibility extended out from her tiny world until the Commons came into view. Lightning danced above and around them, shooting from one end of the sky to the other, but the array of lightning rods prevented direct strikes.

Ash punched open the door and climbed out. She opened the abdomen, relieved to see Hector ready to climb out. He handed her the baby, along with a formula tube. Once she had the little creature, Hector stepped down, wincing with every movement.

"I'm sorry," he said, looking at the sky. "You have to run, Ash. I'll follow as fast as I can."

Ash propped him up as best she could. Wind tugged at her, heralding the end of their brief respite. "I won't leave you," she said.

He pushed her away, fierce determination in his sunken eyes. "You have to," he said. "Get the baby to safety, at least, and then come back for me. Warn the others of..." He trailed off and leaned heavily against the vehicle. "Warn them."

Lightning arced across the sky, followed by a double-crack of bone-shaking thunder. The air smelled of ice and ozone. Ash put her face right up next to Hector's, looking him straight in the eye. "Don't you dare give up," she said, and she kissed him hard on the lips. He was cold at first, but warmth seeped into him as he kissed back. She lingered for the span of a breath, their lips touching.

She ran, feet unsteady in the icy mud. She stuck close to buildings where lightning rods provided the most protection, passing her lab and several houses. Rain pelted her face, but she felt nothing. Cold seeped into every surface of her body, numbing her to the pain. She hugged the baby close, protecting him from the storm.

Wind intensified, and she ran. The last fifty feet were a gauntlet of ice and rain. Ash pushed forward, head down against the abuse. Hail cracked against her head and shoulders, and she shouted—screamed —rage against the elements of Sky. Nothing that world sent at her would keep her from her goal. Not wind, not ice, not even lightning. It crashed around her, playing its wicked dance above the roofs of nearby buildings. Ash didn't slow; didn't dare look back.

She shouldered the door hard, then pounded with a fist. If nobody opened, she would die. Wind tore at her clothes and her flesh, threatening to topple her and sweep her away for good. She pounded on the door again. Could they even hear over the noise of the storm?

The door opened. She handed the baby off to whoever it was, not even caring who. She turned to go help Hector.

Lightning struck the spider. The air shattered with a force that kicked her even from her distance. It blinded her.

When she could see again, Hector wasn't there amongst the scorched wreckage. For a shattered second, she saw the whole path back to the spider, and the big man hadn't followed. He was nowhere to be seen.

Then, silhouetted by a flash of brilliant lightning, Ash saw behind Hector's spider the shape of a much larger vehicle. Dark and sleek, the enormous, many-legged form shrugged off hail like so much salt. Its black windows formed wicked opaque eyes, but Ash knew it must be Marta inside.

Hail surged, driving sideways in the brutal wind. Someone grabbed the back of Ash's coat and pulled her into the building. They shut the door and bolted it closed.

CHAPTER TEN

Ash lay dripping on the cantina floor, herself a puddle among a scattering of ice and mud. She shook from fear and pain, and her numb fingers burned as they warmed. Others surrounded her, and somewhere not far off, the still-nameless baby cried for comfort Ash herself felt she'd never be able to give.

Orson knelt down beside her. "You're okay," he said. "You made it."

Her only answer was to shake her head.

Someone, somewhere declared that the baby needed warm, dry clothes and some formula. Ash agreed silently. Dry clothes sounded nice, but she couldn't summon the strength to ask for anything. How could she? Hector was likely dead, crushed by the storm or by that—woman.

Ash wished she had never helped Marta. It was

a moment of weakness that led her to that cave to help the woman birth a baby that never should have existed. It *had* to end badly. How could she ever think she could cheat the system on a planet with few resources and a brutal climate? Marta should never have tried to produce the modified human. The alien.

Alien. *They* were the aliens, weren't they? They came in peace from a planet far, far away. They brought culture and technology, expecting to dominate the planet and bend it to their will? What kind of hubris did that take? Not only did their ancestors wish to tame an alien world, but they expected to do it without changing themselves. Now, when Marta finally made a person capable of surviving the harsh world, it couldn't survive the inhuman machinations of a generation of humans who lived so many years ago. Maybe none of them would survive the wrath of the AI built hundreds of years ago and set adrift to become the monster that it was.

Who? Who were they to decide who lives or dies? What kind of monster was Traverse to lie and poison and manipulate?

Ash pulled herself up into a sitting position. Someone close spoke in a voice she recognized. Simon. She couldn't understand his words, on account of her head being full of ice. Olympia stood with him at the edge of the crowd.

The bartender gave her a nod, as if he knew she'd be fine all along. Across the cantina, several colonists changed and fed the baby. The bartender took a freshly filled pack out of the machine and slid it down the bar where a man caught it. He handed it to a plump woman in a loose kimono, who cooed quietly and fed the baby. If anybody felt the same uncanny wrongness about the child that Ash did, then they hid it well.

When the baby's crying stopped, Ash's head cleared. It was like tuning a frequency—it snapped into clarity with a bone-shaking suddenness.

"Simon," she said, turning to him. He looked relieved. "We're all in grave danger, and I don't know how to stop it. I don't—I don't even know what it is."

Olympia knelt in front of Ash and looked her straight in the eyes. After a few seconds, she said. "I don't think you have a concussion, but we'd best get some medical techs just in case."

"We don't have time for that," Ash said, rising unsteadily to her feet. "The whole colony is going to collapse. We're going to die if we don't figure it out." She saw the disbelief in Olympia's face. "You have to believe me. We're in danger."

Simon raised an eyebrow and gave the smug look he used when she was being frivolous. "You're telling your story now, right?" he asked. "Where did the baby come from?"

Ash narrowed her eyes at Simon. "He's Marta's baby."

Simon handed her a warm nectar, which she

pushed away. She wanted her head clear. "Marta," he said. "The crazy med tech?"

Olympia elbowed him, hard.

The room swayed under Ash's feet. "She's out there, and she's..." The words failed her. "We can't worry about that right now. Right now, I need to talk to Traverse." She turned to Orson. "Open your display case."

The barkeep looked to Simon, who gave him a quick nod. Orson drew out his keys and opened the case. Ash took Simon's tablet and powered up the device. Traverse's logo spun on the left half, while a readable text interface scrolled along the right. She marveled at the crisp, bright text as it flowed by. Not a single glitch marred the surface.

Ash chewed her lip for a full minute while she came up with a plan. To his credit, Simon sat silently and watched her think. Maybe he detected how serious this was.

"Traverse," she said, pitching her voice loud enough for everyone in the cantina to hear. She felt the pressure of dozens of people looking her direction. "Enter diagnostics mode," she said, and she spoke the override code.

"Override code accepted," Traverse said. On the screen, log data flowed past as Traverse's logo spun.

"Traverse, what is your core mission?"

"As stated by the architects, my mission is to preserve humanity on its journey to the stars."

"Not any individual human?"

"The greater good of humanity's survival is my primary mission." Log data rushed by as he spoke, and Ash leaned in close, so she could watch it. So far as she could tell, she hadn't ventured into any forbidden topics yet, though a few warnings showed that she was close. "Survival of individual humans is secondary."

She had the rapt attention of everyone in the cantina now. Others entered from adjacent rooms, and she suspected that her conversation was being transmitted through the whole building for everyone in the colony to hear.

"Here's a big one, Traverse," she said. "What is humanity?"

"Humanity is the collective of all humans, not only defined by the diversity of their genetics, but the span of their cultures. Humanity is the shared histories of those people on Earth—their stories and their traditions."

Ash let that sink in for a minute; the room hung in silence.

Simon broke the heavy stillness. "What does that even mean? Why is the colony going to collapse?"

Traverse said, "The colony cannot continue when the colonists are all dead."

Ash ran fingers through her wet hair. "Traverse, why are the colonists going to die?"

The cantina broke into a cacophony of voices, panicked an angry, until Ash shushed them all. A wash of warnings scrolled up the diagnostics screen, followed by some overridden errors. She was definitely in forbidden territory with the AI.

"Contamination threatens the overall mission," Traverse said.

"What contamination?"

"Total gestalt has strained the edges of acceptable parameters. Starting generations ago, the people of the ship have been varying from the core definition of humanity. With each change, reevaluation shows more distance from the original genetic and cultural measurements."

Ash set her jaw and spoke very slowly. "What contaminant? Was it something we made in the bio lab? Was it Marta's baby?"

The woman holding the baby gasped and clutched him close.

Traverse didn't speak as the whole colony held a collective breath.

Ash shook the tablet. "Traverse," she said through gritted teeth. "What was the final piece of information that made you decide we were doomed?"

"Humanity's legacy is in its stories and its religions, as well as its genetics," said Traverse in a slow, steady voice. "The stories of Earth are the stories of humanity. Based on the formulated ground truth of all known human works of fiction and nonfiction, the culture of humanity is rooted in those stories. Any story written about extraterrestrial experiences on an alien world must therefore be non-human. As more of those stories are recorded, humanity is reduced. According to procedures, the anomalous colony must be retired and a new colony started."

Ash slumped into a chair. She had suspected the truth, but still couldn't believe it. She pushed the flyer advertising Simon's story contest over to him. "Started a hundred twenty-one days ago. The day Traverse decided to kill us."

Simon's jaw worked back and forth several times before he came up with words. "We're not human because we write stories?" he asked, incredulous. "But that's basically the most human thing we've done here in ages."

"Traverse," Ash said. "What happens if you shut down communications with the ship?"

"The plan will be accelerated, and the colony will be retired immediately."

"How? What do you mean, 'retired?'"

"Solar sails will be shaped to focus sunlight on the affected areas."

The colonists fell into uncontrolled turmoil again, but Ash waved them into silence.

"When will communication with the ship return?" she asked.

"Ten minutes, forty seconds," said the AI.

This time, she didn't try to stop the colonist's chaos. She sat, staring at the wall without another word to say. Over ten minutes, several of the colonists prepared to flee the colony while others tried to convince them that going out into the storm was suicide. The storm roared outside, its constant assault a soothing white noise in the face of their coming death.

"So, this is it?" Simon asked, sitting next to her. "I mean, it won't kill us right away, will it?"

"It will. It'll discover that we found the other colony, and it'll calculate that we need to die right away."

"Other colony?"

She looked at him, half a smile on her face. "There's another colony."

"Huh."

"We might have a few more hours," Ash said. "It'll take time to use the orbital focus to burn us out. I don't think that'll work through the storm unless the ship has a reasonably good angle." There was no way they could stop any of it from the ground. Ash stood, ideas spinning in her head.

Simon's face grew pale. "It's all my fault," he said. "The story contest was my idea."

"Traverse," Ash said. "I would like to speak with my mother as soon as the connection to the ship can be established."

Traverse's logo spun slowly, and the logs still

scrolled by. A small label on the bottom of the screen said "Connecting..."

"If I talk to someone on ship, maybe they can stop the..." She stopped when she saw the word in the logs.

The message on the tablet clearly said, "Simulating..."

"Traverse," Ash said, dread rising in her heart. "What does it mean that it's simulating?"

Traverse did not respond. Several permission errors flew past in the logs.

"Traverse, answer me. I want to speak to my mother."

Again, the simulating message appeared in the logs.

"My *real* mother."

Error messages flew past, succeeded by overrides. Traverse said, "Kamala Morgan has been retired, as support of her biological body was no longer required."

Ash's heart pounded in her chest, and her mouth grew so dry she could hardly speak. "What does that mean?" She exchanged horrified looks with Olympia and Simon. "She moved to the retirement borough three years ago. Are my parents still there?"

"They are no longer in that borough," said Traverse, but the messages told another story. It said, "Retirement borough does not exist."

"Is my mother alive, Traverse? What about my father?"

Simon swooned, and Ash guided him to a chair.

Traverse said, "All past ship residents have been moved to the retirement borough and put to rest. Their voices are simulated for the comfort and well-being of vital colony participants."

Olympia swore. Simon took her hand in his.

"So, they're dead," Ash said. She felt like she was going to vomit. "They've all died, and you've been pretending to be our parents and friends on the ship all along."

Kamala's face appeared on the screen. "That is correct, sweetling."

Ash was about to scream all her rage and futility at the machine when the wall near the door buckled in. The storm surged, and the temperature plummeted. A spike drove through the wall, then another. The whole ten-foot section tore like so much paper, revealing the black spider walker. The front lurched forward, pushing through the segment of wall in a way that disturbingly reminded Ash of the birthing of a child.

Ash shoved Simon and Olympia out of the way, toward the bar. She rushed to the woman holding the baby and took him from her, not bothering to wait for a reaction.

"Go!" Ash shouted over the thunder, waving people toward the door that led further into the Commons. "Everyone, get out!"

But few moved. They stared at the spider as the gigantic head lowered to the floor and opened. Steam hissed off of the giant vehicle's black carapace. Marta stood with a weapon in one hand—a long tube with a glowing end like a flaming torch. She stepped down from the monster's open jaw.

The baby screamed.

CHAPTER ELEVEN

Ash shouted over the storm. "Marta, you need to help us."

Marta leveled her weapon at Ash. She twitched to the side and fired—crack of thunder and rush of heat—the wall behind her had a foot-wide molten hole. "Give me the baby," she said.

Ash pulled the baby close. "You're going to kill him."

"He's mine to kill, Ash." Marta stepped forward, her mad eyes darting from person to person. She sneered at Simon and Olympia as a way to show them that she saw where they hid. "We're all responsible for the monsters we make, whether it's to revel in their glory or despair at their destruction."

"Traverse is the only monster here," Ash said.

"Oh, that's one of them," Marta said. "The AI was set free to rule humanity's journey to the stars. The architects showed us what happens when a monstrosity isn't managed in its infancy. Generation after generation suffered under its rule. Humanity's birth into the stars is an ongoing series of abortions because of their neglect, and I won't repeat that mistake."

"Then destroy the machine. Don't kill your son." Ash stole a step back, closer to the door. "We know Traverse has been killing retired colonists. Our mothers—our fathers are dead because of that monster."

"It's worse than you think. It grew us in our isolated boroughs, like petri dishes incubating the genetic abominations of its latest experiments. Then, when it was close to finding something that might work, it punished us. Cast us aside because we weren't enough like the source material. Burned us."

"No," Ash said. She couldn't believe what Marta said.

"Again, and again, it grew its cultures of not-quite-humans. It planted them on the planet, then burned them with its orbital focus. This is what I learned, connecting to the new colony. Knowledge was always my addiction, and this was its ultimate reward."

"You're wrong, Marta. This baby is not a monster."

"I don't want to kill you, Ash." Her voice grated hard like stone against stone, despite the tears that ran from her eyes. "I don't want any of this, but nobody can live unless that baby dies."

"You don't understand."

Marta let out a frustrated half-animal howl. She leveled her weapon at Ash. "Lies upon lies, Ash." She laughed a laugh devoid of humor. "You regret helping me now, don't you, now that that thing is going to get us all killed." The tip of her weapon glowed, as she held it straight at the baby.

"Traverse," Ash said, not taking her eyes from Marta. "Cut lights."

She ducked to the side as the room plunged into darkness. Marta fired a burnt streak across Ash's vision. Lightning etched dark shapes through the room. Ash ran through the door leading deeper into the building.

Ash pushed through the crowded room on memory alone, her eyes still ruined for darkness by the flash of Marta's weapon. She shouldered one person, then another, the baby cradled tightly in her arms. She needed to get away. Needed time to think or somehow talk to Marta. Or stop her. Or kill her.

All around, people moved in the chaos. Panic pressed closer as she tried to squeeze past. Tension grew in the voices like a mounting reverberation. Its feedback threatened to crush her.

She pushed through, into an open space. On instinct, Ash reached out to find the door to the inner stairs, and she took it. Above, the massive dome let in the cracked light of a broken sky. Yellow flashes showed her the way up, as the baby squirmed and fought in her arms.

The door swung shut behind her, and she rushed upward through the long spiral. She had no plan other than to run, but that was all that was left to her.

When Ash reached the far side of the broad circular staircase, the door burst open. Marta, a furious mess of wet hair and ragged clothing, pointed her weapon across the central open space, and fired.

The bolt hit the outside wall near Ash's head, splashing her with scorching heat. She flinched away and stumbled, the baby twisting in her arms.

"Stay with me, kid," she whispered in its ear. She ran up the stairs, not stopping when her muscles burned, and her lungs ached.

She reached the transparent dome at the top. All above her the sky danced with the anger of heaven above. Edge stretched out below her but driving wind and smashing sleet blocked any view farther than the roof of the building. She could see no farther than the lightning rod scraping the sky high above the Commons roof.

Marta walked up the stairs, her long weapon glowing like a burning torch.

"You've got it wrong, Marta." Ash said to the approaching woman. "Traverse doesn't care about the baby. It's measuring humanity by some antiquated cultural metric. A metric we couldn't possibly fit."

Marta shook her head slowly. "I'd like to believe you, Ash, but it's not true. I was a fool to make that creature, and even if the computer lets us live, it'll be the end of us. That child's people will wipe out humanity on this planet, and there can be nothing of us left."

"Nothing?" Ash said. She walked now, keeping to the side of the dome opposite Marta as the mother stepped onto the upper floor. "He'll have as much as any mother gives her son. He'll have that part of us that is *us*. How can you say he'll have nothing of humanity? Who are you to say that some DNA and a bit of mito-chondrial nonsense are the markers of true humanity?"

Marta said, in a flat voice, "I'm a geneticist."

"And you're wrong. Humanity isn't just the genetics that we've varied from long ago, and it isn't the old stories and cultures from back on Earth. I understand that now. Humanity is something more than that."

Marta raised her weapon, leveling it at Ash.

"Ash!" Simon shouted from below, bursting through the door. Olympia stood beside him, carrying the steel knife in one hand.

Simon threw something at Marta. A fist-sized blue rock struck her arm.

Marta's weapon fired. Ash dove, landing hard on her back to protect the baby. The bolt struck the clear wall, shattering a whole section of the reinforced glass. Wind and rain blasted forth, and the baby screamed in protest.

"Was that the sapphire?" Ash shouted at Simon, aghast. "That came all the way from Earth!"

Marta raised her weapon.

Ash scrambled up and out the window.

Her boots found purchase on the smooth, curved roof. There was nowhere to go, nothing she could do, but she couldn't give up. Ash wouldn't let the baby die by its mother's hand. The raging sky pelted her with everything it had, from bruising hail to freezing rain, and she protected the baby with her body as she lurched forward toward the edge.

Marta stepped onto the roof, weapon held loosely in hand. "You can accomplish a lot when you learn to override the AI's safeties," she said. "It doesn't want us to have weapons, you know. It's afraid we'll hurt our productivity."

Ash didn't have words to respond. She faced the mother, the two women only a few feet apart.

"But isn't war an essential aspect of humanity? Shouldn't Traverse have allowed us to kill each other? What kind of monsters do you think find their way across the stars to subjugate planets? We're not peaceful people, Ash, but our ancestors long ago decided that we should be." She was halfway across the roof now, the wind tearing at her hair. "Maybe they made a mistake when they made Traverse. They told their computer that humanity couldn't change, when in fact humanity *is* change. Always changing, growing, evolving into something different. Something strange." She pointed her weapon at the baby and spoke with contempt. "But not *that* strange."

The baby cried, not a scream at the storm, but the cry of a baby wanting its mother. Its pleading yelps carried through the noise and fury of the world, straight to his mother's ears. Marta hesitated. The tip of the weapon wavered.

Ash kicked the weapon as Marta fired. A pulse of heat lashed out and hit the lightning rod. The rod groaned. Ash grabbed the weapon in one hand trying to wrest it from Marta's grasp. The heat burned Ash's hand.

Marta pulled with both hands, her face a mask of grief and fury.

The rod tipped. Above, black clouds circled, lit by yellow lightning.

Ash kicked at the older woman. A shape moved inside the dome and she thought it might be Simon, but she couldn't look. Marta was stronger and had two hands. Ash couldn't let the woman have the weapon, couldn't let her finally shoot them both.

The lightning rod fell, crashing down between the two women. They flew apart, and Marta's weapon fell from the building. Ash stumbled, feet slipping on the curved roof. She skidded to a halt, dropping to one knee for stability. Marta tumbled farther but came up fast. The air crackled, and Ash's hair prickled.

The building beneath her shook, and her eyes grew wide when she looked down to see what had caused it. Marta's giant black spider moved, extracting itself from the building. Ash turned back to Marta, who now stood at the top of the roof. Simon stayed near the shattered window, but Olympia approached on the slippery roof, knife in hand.

"Give me my baby," Marta said with a voice like gravel. She turned to face Olympia. "You stay out of this."

Olympia feinted with the knife, but Marta stepped up and struck Olympia hard in the jaw. Olympia staggered back, then closed again, more cautious this time.

Ash made her way along the roof, trying to pass back into the building while Marta was distracted. Marta moved to block her path. Olympia, seeing the opportunity, lashed out at the mother with Hector's blade. Steel cut deep into Marta's arm, and blood mixed with the freezing rain.

"You can't have him," Ash shouted over the storm.

"My creation, my responsibility." Marta feinted at Ash, then struck out at Olympia. She wrested the knife from Olympia and kicked the younger girl toward the edge of the roof.

Olympia's feet slipped out from under her, and

she tumbled toward the edge. Simon, now out on the roof, dove for her, catching her arm as she went over the edge.

Ash couldn't help them. "That's not how it works Marta. We're all responsible for this baby's wellbeing. Everybody. The community."

"Are you?" Marta stepped over the fallen lightning rod. "Were you when you left me alone in that cave to fend for myself? When I had to hide my shame from everyone just so that the baby could live? When I starved, alone and cold, waiting for someone to come help me?"

"I did my best." Ash took a step back. She couldn't see Olympia and Simon anymore, and worried they might have fallen over the edge. "Traverse is the real enemy here."

Marta's fists clenched. "Your best wasn't enough." She stepped forward and lashed out with the knife, but Ash stepped back.

Ash's feet skidded on the wet roof. The slope was too much, and she almost couldn't stop. One hand shot out to claw at the rough surface. Marta stood above her, hair whipping in the wind, and lightning-lit clouds framing her face.

"I'm sorry, Ash," she said, and she raised the knife to slash Ash and baby from the edge.

Lightning struck.

Marta's face in her last seconds would be forever burned into Ash's eyes, as lightning pounded into the woman's body through the steel knife and scoured her of life and soul. Electricity pulsed over the roof, blasted through Ash's fingertips, and sent her flying backwards.

Over the edge.

The black spider, large as it was, only reached half the height of the building, even with four of its walking legs leaning against the side, and only two holding it up. Its deft forward arms reached for Ash as she fell, catching her. She stayed there, suspended under the boiling sky for several seconds, holding onto the baby with every ounce of strength she had left.

Then, the spider moved, lowering itself and her down slowly. It maneuvered her so that she entered the building through the gap Marta had left in the wall. It set her down with the grace of a tender lover.

The front of the spider's cabin opened, and Hector stumbled out to collapse on the floor next to her.

Everything went black.

CHAPTER TWELVE

"It's happening," Simon said.

Ash woke to a tumult of panicked voices. She didn't bother to open her eyes for the span of several long breaths. The breaths burned in her lungs and smelled of ash. Not a good sign. She found herself in the medical wing of the Commons, resting in dry, drab clothes on a dry bed. It seemed as good a way to go out as any.

A crib sat nearby, and next to it sat Simon. He looked up as she struggled into a sitting position. Olympia sat next to him, her arm hooked in his. She rested her head on his shoulder, and they looked good together. Comfortable.

Simon let out a sigh. "I don't think there's anything we can do. You might as well lay down and rest."

"You didn't fall to your death," Ash said.

Olympia pulled Simon close. "Thanks to this big, strong guy."

Ash narrowed her eyes. "Wait, was *Simon* the guy who printed gray flowers for you?"

Olympia smiled. "They were nice gray flowers."

Simon's face turned red. "Light blue."

Olympia shook her head but didn't otherwise protest.

The bed next to her held Hector. He stirred, and Ash went to his side and took his hand in hers. He felt warmer even than the room's oppressive heat. Someone had properly bandaged his wounds. The big man would probably live if the whole colony wasn't about to be scorched from Sky's surface.

"Ash," Simon said. "A lot of people took that giant walker and left, but even if they live through the storm, their odds of long term survival out there aren't good without support of the colony."

"We're going to die?" she asked.

Simon nodded.

Ash grabbed hold of his shoulders and shook him. "And you're not even going to *watch* it?" Sometimes Simon made no sense to her at all.

She pushed her way out of the medical wing and down the hallway to the cantina. The woman in the kimono who had so readily accepted the baby sat at one table. Others sat around, awaiting their doom with eerie calm. Ash marveled at the blue-white glow coming through the gaping hole in the wall.

She made her way through the room, and as she passed, attention shifted to her. The band played their reedy instruments: a serenade for death itself.

She stepped outside. A huge second sun burned in the blue sky. It must be the ship, and its focused sunlight scorched away the clouds and disrupted the storm. The air was warm and humid—peaceful as a womb. Her skin ached at the second sun's touch, and after only a minute, started to hurt. She returned to the cantina.

"Traverse," she called out to the tablet still on the table. "The cycle needs to stop." She gave the override code.

Traverse didn't answer for what seemed like an eternity, then it said, "Override code is not accepted. Architect cannot be confirmed."

It used the connection to the ship to verify her identity—not that her override would have helped. It hadn't before. She chewed her lip as Simon and Olympia entered the cantina carrying the baby.

The nameless baby.

After whispering to the band, Ash took the baby from Simon. When their music shifted to a melodic background, she stepped up on stage to share her story.

"Long ago," Ash said, speaking in the best story-telling voice she could manage. "some cultures on Earth wouldn't name their children until they knew they would survive. The mortality rate was so high that they couldn't afford to become attached, sometimes not even until the child was several years old." She spoke to the people in the cantina, but also to Traverse. "This baby's mother, Marta, who we all knew, did not name her child. Whether that was because she feared for his death, or because she thought him a monster, I cannot tell.

"Long ago, the architects of our generation ship designed our future. They created the tools and the machines that would see us live on this new planet. They built an intelligence that would be our guide to the stars and that would see humanity spread throughout the galaxy. They named that intelligence Traverse, because it would traverse the space between worlds, and bring us with it. They named it because they were assured of its survival. It was their greatest creation and it was to be their key to immortality.

"But these architects did not know what it was to be human. In their hubris they fed their machine everything they knew, of cultures and genetics. They gave it the very best they could of what they were. Traverse, you were formed of a flawed ideal. You thought humanity was defined by what it *was*. Humanity is so much more.

"The architects never named our people. They never gave those travelers who would voyage out into the stars a proper name. They thought of us as an extension of themselves. We were to be like them, and they expected us to stay that way." Ash gestured at the baby. "But this child. This creation.

He is the future of us. That is a human adapted to *this* world. The child can live a long life on Sky, breathing its air and thriving in its climate. He is the natural progression of us as *we* adapt to the new world."

Ash panted, the effort of telling her story taking the burning breath from her lungs. "This is the start of his story, and his story is as human as it gets. He is the adventurer in an uncharted world. He is the first of many. He is the chosen one, and so long as he and his descendants live, so must this world. So, must this colony."

She stood in silence a long time. Outside, the light increased, as waves of heat scorched away the last of the puddles.

"Traverse," Ash said, unable to keep the quake of fear from her voice. "The definition of humanity needs to split. Your old definition is for Earthlings, and they are light years away. We here are Skylings, and this." She raised the baby high above her head. "*This* young child is Skye, the first of our people."

The room held another long silence on the edge of a knife. The music drew long into a tense transition.

Ash stalked to the opening in the wall and shouted up at the sky. "His story has only started! This is the first chapter, and he needs to live. We Skylings need to live!" The musicians picked up her intensity.

Heat burned the sky and earth, rising in waves

from the ground. At the edge of town, a wall of storm swirled around the open air, crashing at the burning sky with its darkest fury. Lightning scraped across the storm wall like the claws of a ravenous beast.

"It's time to be done with the lies, Traverse. Time to stop this vicious cycle. How many colonies have you printed and destroyed? We're not going to be more like the Earthlings, no matter what you do, and you know what? We don't want to be. We have our own stories to tell, and our own battles to fight. Skylings are human, Traverse." Tears streamed down her face. "This is as human as it gets."

The air burned her lungs, but through it all Skye stayed silent and alert. His world burned as he watched. He drew scalding air through his nose flaps and looked up at Ash with wide, dark eyes. How had she ever thought him ugly or unsettling? All she saw in her arms was a perfect baby. Perfect and strange. The music stopped.

"Definition accepted," Traverse said.

The light in the sky dimmed, and clouds crept greedily forward to close the gap. Over several minutes, the storm returned with its full vengeance, as if offended at their brief reprieve. Ash ignored the colonists' cheers, handed the baby off to another colonist, and showed herself back to her bed in the medical wing where she collapsed into a deep sleep.

CHAPTER THIRTEEN

"YOURS WAS A PRETTY GOOD STORY," Simon said. He tossed Ash the penny.

He, Olympia, Hector, and Ash walked outside for the first time in several days. Olympia held Simon's hand, and Ash hooked arms with Hector. The big man leaned on her from time to time, but his wounds were healing well. The ashen gray sky threatened to burst again, but all of the forecasts from the ship showed that the last arm of the storm's spiral wouldn't sweep over them for another few hours.

Ash said, "It wasn't really a story at all. I tried to come up with something but gave up and asked the stupid computer for help."

Simon chuckled. "I did that for my story, too, and I don't think it's cheating." He had won the contest by vote of the colonists. He'd written a good story, and its delivery had kept the colonists entertained for an entire day. "But your story saved the colony, and that counts for something, right?"

They passed Hector's ruined spider. Ash tugged Hector to keep him from trying to walk to it. He turned to her, and she planted a kiss on him before he could say anything. She spoke with their lips gently brushing. "We'll meet you back here," she said. "Soon."

He smiled. "Thanks." The big man limped to his spider walker and started doing whatever it is men do with broken hunks of construction equipment. Mourn, Ash supposed.

She said to Simon, "Is it true the ship is going to send more colonists?"

"Yeah," Simon said. "That's what they're saying. Nobody knows if we can trust the ship anymore. It lied about people still being alive. Even our families and friends. Turns out all along, when people hit retirement age they die, and the ship simulates them. The AI wouldn't stand for people who might draw resources without contributing."

Ash shuddered. She tried not to think of all the ways the ship had deceived them, but every day they found something new. "I think about what happened to Marta's lover. She became dangerous, so Traverse poisoned her."

Simon nodded, grim look on his face.

Ash said, "It moved the bulk of our feedstock to the new colony. I don't think it's going to give that back." The colonists who had fled with the giant spider had eventually returned with the supplies they'd taken, but it wasn't much.

They walked in silence for a while, circling through the colony and surveying the damage. It wasn't bad, but a few of the smaller buildings had toppled under the storm. A great pressure lifted from Ash's chest when she saw her lab was still in good shape. She steered toward it, as if drawn.

The lights activated as they entered the building, and for a moment, Ash had a vision of the lab in the other colony. This place was her home, but somehow everything had changed in her memory. She remembered clean tables and polished floors, but here, everything was covered in a greenish-blue grime.

Olympia let out a sigh. "What is this all over everything?" She ran to her side of the lab bench and started organizing her things. "Ugh, there's stuff all over."

Ash removed her rebreather and pulled in deep breath. The air was sweet and warm, and it felt good in her lungs. Breathing it made her acutely aware of how difficult Sky's air was on her. They'd learned to accommodate to the planet's atmosphere, but that didn't mean they were perfectly attuned to it.

Then, she saw their incubator.

"What happened?" Simon asked.

The incubator was covered in a green powder with black spores floating like dust in the harsh lights. Spores covered the incubator, inside and out.

That accounted for the grime covering her old lab and the filth all over Olympia's equipment. She touched a spot on the lab bench, drawing away a finger covered in spores.

"It's my terraforming project," she said. "It's the first step that will make this world habitable."

"Won't that make it a harder place for Skye to live?"

She shook her head. "No. It'll be even better for him than it is for us. Marta thought of that in her designs. I've tried to understand what she did, and most of it's beyond me, but that much is pretty clear. She designed for change, and the Skylings will be better for it."

"Seems like she had one up on the architects if she designed expecting change."

"She was brilliant," Ash said. She pried open the incubator and removed the original petri dish with her specimen. The dish itself was barely recognizable under the mass of algae-like substance.

Ash flipped Simon the penny. "You earned this, Simon, and I don't think I need a penny any more. The Earthlings had a lovely world, but I think it's time to build our own."

"You still want my tablet, though, don't you?"

"I will fight you for that thing."

Simon wisely chose not to fight.

Ash lifted the tray of algae and carried it to the door.

"Are you sure about this?" Simon asked. She

didn't know if he was referring to the penny or the thriving microorganisms.

"Our story's still in the first chapter," Ash said, "so I'm not sure about anything."

She opened the door and cast the organism out into the world, sending its spores high into the atmosphere for the trailing edge of the storm to spread to all the corners of Sky.

EPILOGUE

Finn Schmidt didn't like it one bit.

He rolled up the sleeves of his gray coveralls and eyed the replacement lightning rod. The long, metal shaft lay atop a customized spider walker on the vast floor of the Fabricator building, fully tested and awaiting installation. This antenna was finally ready to replace the destroyed lightning rod.

The fixture shouldn't even have needed replacement, but the storm had mangled the old one. That meant long hours for his engineering crew and incessant, unending requests for improvements and modifications from ill-advised scientists.

"I'm just saying," said Max, the absolute worst physicist in the entire colony, "we could do a lot better." Max's long, gray lab coat brushed the floor as he gestured with his stick arms. "A molecular emitter. Think about it."

"No."

"An emitter could deliver the contents of any molecular biopack to the entire colony instantly. It could save us all in case of a medical emergency."

"That's not what you have planned." Finn stepped back from the antenna and pressed a button on his control tablet. The walker extended its legs and rose from the ground.

Max chewed his lip. "I might—"

"No. You plan on cramming cookies or rotten fruit into it or something like that." He pressed another button and the giant double doors of the Fabricator opened to let in the cool night air. Finn walked alongside the antenna as it passed outside. He fixed his rebreather in place, making sure it had a good seal.

"What about medicine." Max strolled alongside Finn, wind snapping at his lab coat.

"It is a terrible idea and can't possibly pass safety testing."

They walked in silence for a while, the spider thumping along heavily on the rough cobblestones. They passed Simon, the handsome guy who worked in the Archives. Max started toward him, but Finn held out an arm to stop him.

"He's dating someone now," Finn said.

"Oh." Max's shoulders slumped.

"So are you."

"It's an open relationship," Max said. "Did you hear Edge might run out of food?"

Finn pinched the bridge of his nose. "What?"

"Yeah, all our foodstock went over to that new colony."

"Nobody lives there," said Finn. He adjusted his spider's gait so it would move a little faster through the empty street. He could see the Commons looming against the starlit sky. "We can just go get it back."

"Yeah." Max deflated again.

"What? What's wrong with that? The colony is empty and they're not going to need our food."

"I was hoping to try some new modifications to the recycler."

Finn peered at his friend. "What?"

"The fusion core can be configured to collect certain atomic substances, right? Well, what if we could give it granite and have it spit out..."

When Max trailed off, Finn said, "You don't want to say it, do you? You just realized it was the stupidest in a long line of stupid things, and you're embarrassed to mention it because you know I'll make fun of you. It's going to be something dangerous and ill-advised. You're talking about configuring a dangerous nuclear reactor so that it eats granite and spits out radioactive snacks or some such. The emitter is something you foresee as an easy way to deliver a cure for radiation sickness."

Max said nothing.

"Am I right?"

Max pointed at the sky, where a streak of light departed from the millions of stars. It danced through the upper atmosphere and shone against the dusky red backdrop of one of Sky's seven moons. "A shuttle," he said.

They watched in silence as the shuttle arced through the sky. It veered toward Edge.

"We're not scheduled to get more colonists," said Finn.

But the shuttle turned. It banked over the ocean and disappeared into the distance.

Toward the other colony.

"So much for getting our food back," said Finn.

"What do you think about calling it a Snacku-factory?"

"No."

"Like manufactory, but for snacks."

"Yeah, I got it."

Max slapped Finn on the back. "I knew you'd like it."

At the Commons, the spider stopped at the side of the building. One by one, Finn switched its feet for better climbers. The default feet would manage just fine, but he liked his ratios better with customized claw hooks. As he worked on the change, several colonists emerged from the Common's building carrying what looked like a hideous baby.

"I thought you were joking about that," Finn muttered after the group had left.

"I never joke," said Max. "Mutant babies are cool now. Get with the times, man."

Finn shrugged. The child's oddities didn't bother him but violating the population cap was always trouble. He glanced at a spot not far away, where someone had died from a lightning strike. He felt a mixed pang guilty satisfaction at the thought of it balancing the numbers. This was the worst tragedy since Finn had arrived on Sky, but things happen when people don't obey basic safety precautions. What was she doing up on the roof during the storm, anyway? "Well, at least we're still strict about what you scientists are allowed to unleash into the world."

Max didn't say anything, but Finn could tell. He could *just* tell.

Gesturing for Max to follow him into the Commons, Finn said, "Out with it."

"One of the biologists released something from the biolab."

The floor in the Commons was wet and slick with slime. Dangerous working conditions, if ever Finn saw them. Still, he didn't want to leave without finishing this job. He ascended the stairs, careful to hold tight to the railing.

"The claim is that her biological agent will scrub the atmosphere," Max said, following Finn. "It might work, too."

"Or it might not. Did they test that it would work? Did they check for dangerous byproducts? I hope it didn't spread far so that we can monitor this organism's development."

"She released it in the heart of the storm so that it would spread across the whole planet quickly."

Finn might have pulled out his hair in frustration, but he didn't want to let go of the railing. At the top of the Commons, under the dome, shattered glass crunched under his feet where a loose tarp flapped over a broken hole, failing entirely at its intended task of keeping the elements out. "This is ridiculous."

Max tore open the tarp and stepped out onto the slick roof. "This is perfect!" he cried.

Finn's heart slammed in his chest, but he choked back the words reprimanding Max about safety because he knew it would just get him mocked. "Be careful out there." Almost.

Max barked out a laugh and danced a jig. "You can make that shattered spot into a door and we'll build an emitter chamber here. The antenna can attach to it, and we'll be able to make the whole colony smell like whatever we want."

Finn clipped his safety tether to the railing and stepped out onto the roof. He had to admit that he could see Max's vision. A chamber would fit there. "We'll have to check the roof supports."

"Sure, sure, sure." Max spread his arms and twirled on the curved roof.

Finn punched some controls on his tablet, and the spider started its climb up the Commons wall. After a minute, it emerged onto the roof, the antenna still affixed to its back. It settled itself in place next to the old mounting brackets where several feet of mangled lightning rod still stood.

Finn used his multitool to start removing the old hardware. "This doesn't *look* like storm damage," he said.

"Did you hear about the story contest?" Max asked as he circled the spider. His foot slipped, and even though he didn't fall, Finn's heart made another leap for his throat. "Whoa that was close. Anyway, I guess Simon won."

"Wasn't it *his* contest?" A bolt came free and the mangled remains of the antenna tilted to one side.

"He's probably the smartest guy on the planet, so I guess he was bound to win." Max draped an arm over Finn's shoulder. "He's like a skinny, sexy dictionary."

"He's in a relationship," Finn said.

Max waved it away like a pestering fly. "That doesn't mean I appreciate him any less."

"Some people don't want to be appreciated."

"Jealous?"

Finn swore as the second bolt came free. The twisting of the old rod pulled hard against the base. "Have you forgotten about Sonya?"

"You going out with her tonight?"

"Maybe tomorrow." He poked the final bolt with his multitool. The head was bent, which didn't bode well for the threads coming out unstripped. "Anyway, put some pressure on this."

The way the old lightning rod had melted on

one side and then broken off as it fell had done a lot of damage to its base. More than Finn had seen when he had first inspected the site. With Max pulling as hard as he could, pressure lifted from the final bolt, and Finn was able to move it a couple of turns.

"I bet if I get the Snacufactory working, Traverse will let us increase the colony's population."

Finn's tool slipped and he barked his knuckles on the antenna.

"Maybe this'll be a city someday," said Max.

"Not in our lifetimes."

"No, really, I think it could. You're right, though, we'll have to stop feeding people radioactive food." He gazed at the starry sky. "There are so many people living up on the ship who would be great down here. Plus, think how fast we could accelerate our research if we had more scientists."

Finn ground his teeth and pushed, but the bolt wouldn't budge.

"Incidentally, the dating pool would increase."

With a shout, Finn finally moved the bolt. Bolt, lightning rod, and Max all tumbled toward the edge of the roof.

Finn lunged, grabbed Max's wrist, and reeled him in. The rod crashed to the ground below, prompting several angry shouts.

"Sorry," Finn called out, guilt tightening his

chest. What if someone had gotten hurt? "I'll try to be more careful."

"You're *way* too careful already," said Max, as if *too careful* were actually a thing.

The night went quiet. Above, the moons made their long journey across the sky. With a few swipes at the controls, Finn guided the new antenna into position. With Max's help, he attached the new hardware. When the job was finished, he sat on the crown of the roof and watched the stars.

Max sat next to him. "Look," he said in the most serious voice Finn had ever heard from the scientist. "I know you just want everyone to be safe."

"What I don't understand," said Finn, "is why everyone else doesn't want to *be* safe."

Max grinned under his rebreather and the grin made his eyes sparkle. "That wouldn't be much fun, though, would it?"

They sat for a while with nothing but the whisper of the gentle wind as their muse. Finn gazed at the sky, trying to find the trail of the shuttle they had seen moving toward the other colony. It was gone, erased from the sky as if it had never been there.

"Cities have their own problems," he finally said, almost to himself.

"Like what? Night clubs? Social gatherings? A variety of food? What terrible danger do you foresee in the colony of Edge?"

"Crime," said Finn. "Murder."

"You are so pessimistic."

"I'm a realist."

"You know what comes with murder, right?"

"No, what?"

"Brilliant investigators."

Finn pushed himself to his feet and made his way back into the building. "You really think we'll have any of those? Who around here could possibly investigate a murder?"

"I don't know," said Max. "How about that biologist who just unleashed an organism into the upper atmosphere."

"That's the worst idea you've had all week, and I'm including the radioactive Snackufactory."

A mischievous grin flashed across Max's face. "It would keep her out of trouble."

"Would it, though?" Finn sighed and detached his tether. "Well, come on then."

"What? Where are we going?"

"Downstairs for a drink." He slapped his friend on the back. "If this colony is going downhill, it's up to us to figure everything out over drinks."

"Channeling your anxiety for good?"

Finn was careful on the glass-strewn stairs, careful on the slick landing below, and careful all the way into the cantina where he carefully ordered himself the largest nectar Orson would give him. The day's job was finished, and it was time to enjoy life for a while in the colony of Edge.

AUTHOR'S NOTE

Author's Note

Thank you all for reading Of a Strange World Made.

A special thanks goes out to my wife Carol and my boys Isaac and Gabe. Without their support I would never have gotten this book written, edited, and published.

Huge thanks go out to my Beta Readers. You've helped make this story the best it can be and I'm eternally grateful.

Thanks go out to Scott Alexander Jones for fantastic editing that always seems to find ways to improve everything I write.

-Anthony W. Eichenlaub